WITH ALL MY LOVE

It's 1962, and Jacqueline is fighting the temptation to ignore moral standards and conventions with her fiancé, Chris. Confused by her conflicting feelings, she accepts the offer of a three-week working holiday in Switzerland. Away from home and the steadying influence of Chris, she finds herself desperately attracted to the handsome Antoine. Jackie, still deeply in love with Chris, holds out against Antoine's charms — but then an unlucky skiing accident undermines her good intentions . . .

*Books by Patricia Robins
in the Linford Romance Library:*

THE FOOLISH HEART
SAPPHIRE IN THE SAND
TOPAZ ISLAND

PATRICIA ROBINS

WITH ALL MY LOVE

Complete and Unabridged

LINFORD
Leicester

First published in Great Britain in 1963

First Linford Edition
published 2010

British Library CIP Data

Robins, Patricia, 1921 –
   With all my love.- -(Linford romance library)
   1. Vacations- -Switzerland- -Fiction.
   2. Skiing accidents- -Fiction.
   3. Love stories. 4. Large type books.
   I. Title II. Series
   823.9'14–dc22

   ISBN 978–1–84782–987–0

Published by
F. A. Thorpe (Publishing)
Anstey, Leicestershire

Set by Words & Graphics Ltd.
Anstey, Leicestershire
Printed and bound in Great Britain by
T. J. International Ltd., Padstow, Cornwall

This book is printed on acid-free paper

1

Jackie watched her fiancé as he opened the door to let her mother pass through with the empty coffee cups and felt a surge of pride, love and longing sweep through her. Chris was always so thoughtful. He was switching on the hall light now — following Mum into the kitchenette, and no doubt he would stay and wipe the cups and saucers.

'You're tired, darling!' he'd said a moment ago. 'You stay put. I'll be back in a moment.'

Jackie leant her dark chestnut-coloured head against the cushions on the worn old sofa and closed the greeny-grey eyes which were her best feature. She *was* tired. It had been a full day at Moulin's — the hairdressing shop where she was Number 1 assistant. Two perms and a trim before lunch — two sets and finally the imperious Veronica Cairgorn for a bleach and set. Mrs. Cairgorn was their wealthiest client and Jackie and the other girls had nicknamed her 'My Lady' because she was so demanding and exacting.

But although Jackie's slim young body was tired, her mind remained strangely active and her thoughts followed the young fair-haired, blue-eyed man to whom she was engaged.

Darling Chris! He'd be back soon and they'd be alone — for Mum would go up to bed early as she usually did when Chris came to supper — being tactful, she called it! Chris would come across the room and kiss her and then . . .

Jackie's eyes opened suddenly and she stared thoughtfully into the fire-light. And then, what? A frown creased the smooth young forehead and her long slim, beautifully-manicured fingers twisted together in her lap. These sessions alone with Chris had begun to be a bit of a problem. During the first year of their engagement Chris had been the passionate, demanding lover, kicking against the reins of convention that placed limitations upon their lovemaking. She had been the one contented just to be kissed, caressed and held in his strong young arms. And then, last Christmas, they had nearly lost control . . .

Jackie could not forget that brief moment before they forced themselves to stop before it was too late. It was the first time she had fully understood the tremendous force of mutual passion. She was frightened and at the same time exalted. She began to think of marriage as something more than a white bridal gown, wedding presents and a gold band on her finger to proclaim her new status as a wife. She realized that these were only the merest formalities, and that beneath the trimmings she would be dedicating herself — body as well as soul, to the man she loved.

The honeymoon no longer meant

some kind of glorified holiday to be discussed and planned. It was a time set aside from ordinary living when she and Chris would have to know each other with no secrets left.

She was not afraid of this — her body craved the fulfilment at present denied them. She was only afraid of the temptation — never far from her thoughts since that night — that *she* might not be strong-minded enough to stop Chris if the moment were to be repeated.

Perhaps if she could have explained her feelings to Chris her emotions would have seemed right and normal. But he had reacted so strangely — almost as if he felt guilty for showing how passionately he wanted her. Their first time alone together afterwards he had apologized, accusing himself of momentary madness, of weakness. He'd made it painfully obvious that he was thoroughly ashamed of himself. Because she did not feel ashamed, she felt guilty. Yet deep down inside, she didn't see why she should feel guilty. After all, she and Chris were going to be married. It was right they should want each other in every way.

They'd been dating since grammar school days when they'd first fallen in love. There'd never been anyone else for either of them and there never would be. Jackie couldn't bring herself to believe that they had nearly succumbed through weakness. It seemed to her it was the strength of their need for one another which had been so hard to resist.

Lately, their hours alone together had been clouded by Chris's iron determination not to take any risks which might tempt them too near the fire again. Their attitudes had become reversed. Chris, it seemed, was content now with mere kisses, and Jackie was the one who was torn with a desire to be as loving as possible to the man she loved.

'We must be sensible!' Those words were constantly on Chris's lips and constantly on her nerves. Chris's behaviour was almost puritanical — especially when Jackie considered the behaviour of those around them. Rona, the manicurist at Moulin's, had been living with her boyfriend quite openly for years. Not that Jackie herself approved, any more than she approved of the way several of the girls at the shop messed around with every Tom, Dick and Harry, completely disregarding social conventions. But she and Chris were genuinely in love. Surely it was not wrong to lie in each other's arms, kissing and embracing as much as they both wished, provided they knew when to stop. They *were* going to be married — just as soon as they could afford to buy the house they wanted.

Jackie sat up and stretched her arms above her head and sighed again. The only really *sensible* thing would be to get married right away. That's what *she* would like to do, but Chris didn't agree.

'You look absolutely smashing tonight.'

Chris came across the room, sat down beside her on the sofa and took her in his arms. 'A penny for them, darling, or has the price gone up?'

She threw her arms round his neck and put her face against his cheek.

'I was thinking of you — of us. Kiss me.'

She was quite unconsciously seductive as she pressed her slim young body closer against his. For a moment his arms tightened about her and his kiss was as hard and demanding and full of passion as she wished it to be. Then he gently pulled her arms away and held them down against her side.

'We must be sensible, darling.'

His voice was full of tenderness, but it left her with a sudden cold, painful feeling of hate. She felt a quite primitive desire to slap his face — hard. Instead, she turned away from him and said in an angry little voice,

'It's been a bloody awful day.'

She sensed rather than saw Chris stiffen beside her. She very rarely swore and she knew he hated it.

'That ghastly woman, Mrs. Cairgorn, was in and made things just about as damn difficult for everyone as she could.'

'But I thought you rather liked her?' Chris said, perplexed by the sudden change in her. Sometimes he didn't understand Jackie at all. One moment she would be soft and sweet and utterly feminine, and then as now, hard and unapproachable. He wanted to hold her hand, to bring her close to him again, but he knew when she was in one of these moods that she would only take her hand away.

For a moment or two she didn't reply, and then she turned and said:

'Chris, let's get married.'

'But, darling . . .'

His voice trailed away uncertainly. Obviously, Jackie was serious; her eyes, her outstretched hands, her whole body, expressed an urgent appeal. He knew he must not make a flippant reply; he couldn't give her a flat 'no,' either. But she knew they couldn't afford to get married yet.

Watching his face, Jackie guessed his thoughts — Chris being sensible again.

'Well, *why not?*' she demanded suddenly, furiously and childishly annoyed with him. 'Why should we go on wasting the best years of our lives just because of a blasted house?'

He looked as shocked as she had meant him to be. One-half of her felt slight pity for him. She had, after all, been in complete agreement with him when they'd discussed the future the day they became engaged. They'd jointly agreed that since they were both young there was no point in rushing into an early marriage. Apart from anything else, they hadn't enough money. Since her father had died, Jackie had contributed to the upkeep of the semi-detached house she and her mother shared. Mum couldn't afford to stay in it if those contributions stopped.

Then there was Chris's position. He'd been brought up in a rather ugly, overcrowded house in a row in the middle of Bickley, the neighbouring suburb. His father had worked for British Railways and there'd never been enough money to pay for the needs of the six children who'd been crowded into the terraced house. Four years ago Chris's mother, whom he loved dearly, had died. She'd always had a weak heart, and the hard struggle to bring up her family, for whom she was constantly sacrificing herself, was too much for her. Jackie knew that Chris was determined that *her* life would be different. He'd never had a chance to improve his mother's lot, for he'd only just qualified as a bank accountant. He'd worked hard throughout school and during his training, so that he could repay some of his mother's early sacrifices, and then she'd died before he could realize that ambition. Jackie was mature enough to appreciate that Chris had transferred all his enthusiasms to her, and she respected him for the strength of character which had got him a much better job than his father had ever had.

She knew it was unfair to complain now about Chris's commonsense and reliability, since these traits among others had first attracted her to him. Mentally she accepted the fact that Chris was right to want a nice house, nicely furnished, with a little money in the bank before they married. It was her heart which was crying out against the frustration of being so close to him yet never quite close enough.

Chris said, breaking the silence:

'We shouldn't have to wait so very much longer, darling. I've brought the little black book with me. Would you like to have a look at it?'

She hesitated. She didn't really want to discuss finances, and yet she knew what the 'little black book' meant to Chris. He produced it now, opened it on his lap and pointed to the neat columns of figures.

'Look, Jackie. We've six hundred pounds in our savings account. Another hundred will pay the twenty per cent down-payment on the kind of house we want. Incidentally, darling, I saw one in last night's evening paper at just our price — three thousand two-fifty. Then there are the legal fees and stamp duty — that shouldn't come to more than thirty pounds. If we cut down a bit on the furniture — perhaps only do the living room and bedroom and kitchen — we might be able to think in terms of next autumn.'

'Maybe we won't feel like getting married next autumn.'

She knew the remark was perverse.

She wondered, suddenly suppressing a giggle, if she were becoming schizo-phrenic, if there weren't sometimes two of her — one the loving, easy-going, contented girl whom Chris loved; the other a rather bitchy woman who wanted to hurt him because *she* felt hurt. Everything Chris said made sense. Everything he did was for her, for their joint happiness. She knew it wasn't fair to accuse him of putting pounds, shilling and pence before love, and yet at moments like these, face to face with the little black book, that was how it seemed.

Chris's blue eyes looked at her with cold surprise.

'You've changed, Jackie. You never used to talk this way.'

It was almost a quarrel — and they never quarrelled. Jackie was suddenly frightened. Impulsively, she threw herself back into his arms and said:

'Sorry, darling. You know I didn't really mean that. I expect I'm just tired and on edge. Forgive me?'

He softened at once and planted a kiss on the tip of her nose.

'Of course, and you do look tired, darling. Perhaps I ought to go.'

'No, no, please don't. I'm all right, really. Besides, I haven't had a chance to tell you what happened at the shop today . . .'

She hadn't really intended to tell him about Veronica Cairgorn's fantastic invitation, but now she was anxious to detain Chris. It was only ten o'clock and she knew if she went up to bed she wouldn't sleep, tired as she was.

'She actually suggested I go to Switzerland with her in a fortnight's time. I think the idea was that I should be a sort of glorified hairdresser-cum-maid-cum-companion. She knows I speak French fluently, because I told her Father was half-Swiss and that we lived in Geneva until after the war. She even went so far as to ask Mr. Paul if he'd let me go. Of course she's frantically rich, and I've no doubt she offered Mr. Paul compensation. Do you know, Chris, she was prepared to pay all my expenses plus my normal salary and a fifty-pound bonus into the bargain. I might say I was jolly well tempted for a few moments.'

'Tempted! I should say so. You didn't refuse, did you, Jackie?'

She looked at him in amazement.

'But of course I did. It was for three whole weeks, Chris. I wouldn't want to be away from you for so long.'

'But, darling . . . ' He hesitated, frowning. 'Of course, it's sweet of you to think of me, and I should hate you being away, but surely under the circumstances it is sheer madness not to accept an offer like that. You're badly in need of a holiday after that bout of 'flu last month, and what a holiday! Why, you could even do some ski-ing again and you'd love that, wouldn't you? Besides, her offer's a very generous one. Do you realize that fifty-pound bonus would cover the legal fees and stamp duty on our house, and leave something over? You didn't really refuse, did you, Jackie?'

She got up and walked across to the window. She stared out into the street — looking without seeing. She *had* refused. The first moment of temptation had soon given way to the certainty that even in Switzerland she would be utterly miserable parted from Chris for three long weeks. She'd told Veronica Cairgorn as much, and although the woman seemed disappointed she'd accepted

Jackie's reason as if she fully appreciated her feelings. Was that because despite her rather hard brittle manner, she was still a woman at heart? Did it need a woman to understand feminine psychology? Obviously Chris didn't. He thought she was stupid to put sentiment first. She felt oddly humiliated, as well as angered by his attitude. It was certainly not what she'd expected. Chris should have said, 'But I couldn't bear to be parted from you either.'

Maybe she was being stupidly romantic. Maybe in time she'd look upon Chris's unexpected reaction as both sensible and unselfish.

Tears filled her eyes and spilled over down her cheeks. She tried to stop them, but they kept coming. Normally she never cried. The last occasion had been six years ago when her father had died. She'd been fifteen. She remembered now the noisy sobbing that had brought her a sense of relief. These tears were different — brought on by over-tense nerves and unconscious frustration.

'Darling, what on earth's the matter?'

Chris was horrified to see her wet cheeks, and at once began to dry them with his handkerchief, with ineffectual masculine awkwardness.

Some of the tension went out of her body, and although the tears still dripped from the end of her nose she no longer wanted to weep. Poor Chris — poor darling! He simply didn't understand, and the anxious questions and endearments poured from his lips and reawakened all the love and tenderness she felt for him.

'I'm sorry!' she whispered. 'You're probably right, I do need a holiday. Couldn't we go away together, Chris? If we could both get a week off perhaps we could go down to Clacton.'

'But you know I can't get off till June, Jackie. I'm not due for leave until then. I suppose I might ask for it on compassionate grounds, but I don't think the manager would like it, and I don't even know if your illness would be adequate grounds for compassionate leave. If — '

He broke off, uncertain as to whether it would be tactful to mention the subject, but Jackie knew exactly what he intended to say — *If we were married it would be different.*

'That's about the fact of the matter,' Jackie thought. 'If we were married there'd be no question of my going away without Chris. Well, I suppose I might as well go to Switzerland if Mrs. Cairgorn hasn't found anyone else. Chris seems to think I'd be silly if I don't accept the offer, and after all, it *might* be fun.'

After he had kissed her good night and left, still a little anxious about her, Jackie lay in bed and thought about Veronica Cairgorn. Undoubtedly she would expect Jackie to earn the money she was to be paid for her services, but Jackie didn't mind that. She'd never been afraid of hard work. At the same time, she wasn't sure if she could put up with the older woman's rather hard, strident voice and dictatorial manner for three whole weeks. Of course, she was a very attractive woman with turquoise-blue eyes that were quite startling and classical features. A discontented droop to a thin mouth spoiled what was otherwise an arresting face. She used all the known beauty aids and frequent massage and diet had helped to keep her beautiful figure. She was always gorgeously dressed. Her clothes came from houses like Balmain, Balenciaga, Dior. She sometimes came into the shop wearing the most beautiful sapphire mink. Seeing things through Chris's eyes, Jackie realized that this one coat would no doubt pay the deposit on the house they wanted!

Her last thought before she fell asleep was whether men found the beautiful Veronica irresistible, and if so, whether Chris would have found it quite so easy to be sensible with Veronica as he was with her.

2

'You are a lucky so-and-so, Jackie,' Rona said enviously as the two girls took a brief moment of respite in the small cubicle which served Paul Moulin's assistants as a rest room.

Jackie took the kettle off the gas-ring and gave her friend a quick smile. They had no secrets from each other, and Jackie said now:

'I'd be much more excited if I were going with Chris. Honestly, Rona, I don't understand men. Chris says he's madly in love with me, yet he actually spent half last night talking me into going away from him for three weeks.'

She stirred in the coffee powder and handed a cup to Rona.

'It'll be different when you've gone — he'll find out then just how much he misses you. Just you wait and see.'

'Absence makes the heart grow

fonder, you mean,' Jackie said with a rueful smile. 'Rona, would you go — and leave Pete?'

'It's different for me — as you know, we're living together.'

'Yes,' thought Jackie, 'you belong to him. I don't belong to Chris like that. He doesn't seem to want it particularly — but I do. Mum would have a fit if she knew what I thought. In a way, I admire Chris for sticking to conventions. How I wish we were already married and could forget them!'

'You've picked a man with principles!' Rona said, as if she'd been following Jackie's train of thought.

'I know! I don't think I want him different — or really want to take our relationship a stage further until we are married. It's just that I want him to want me. Do you know what I mean, Rona? His attitude seems so half-hearted, as if he were only half in love with me.'

Rona nodded her red head.

'Sex!' She gave the one word a wealth

of meaning. 'I suppose it is for some 'the root of all evil.' Anyway, Jackie, seeing how things are between you, I'd say three weeks apart is a jolly good idea. You've been engaged far too long — seeing each other every day — it's gone stale on you. You know what all the women's magazines say about long engagements. I think they are a mistake, too.'

'That's really the trouble,' Jackie thought, as young Sue, the apprentice, came into the little room, making further conversation impossible. 'Chris and I ought to get married. If we go on like this I'll end up a nervous wreck and not able to love Chris at all.'

For the rest of the day Jackie tried to stop thinking about her emotions and concentrate on her work. She had a natural talent for hairdressing, and, apart from Mr. Paul, was most in demand by their customers. The women liked her quiet, rather low-pitched voice, and admired her looks. She was attractive in a cool, fresh way, her eyes a lovely grey-green fringed with dark lashes, and her skin a natural creamy-white which glowed when she wore the more pinky tones of lipstick.

Jackie was popular with the other girls, too. Unlike them, she refused to become involved in petty jealousies and was always willing to help out if things got rushed, although she was accepted as senior assistant and was in charge when Mr. Paul was on holiday.

Mr. Paul was an exacting but fair employer. Provided the girls did their work well and kept the salon tidy and attractive, he didn't boss them around. But he could bark pretty fiercely if they left a customer too long under the drier or he found a dirty basin or mirror.

In the lunch break Jackie telephoned Veronica Cairgorn to find out if the invitation to accompany her to Switzerland was still going.

'But of course — and I'm thrilled you've changed your mind. No one does my hair just like you — not even my London girl. Then it's definite you'll come?'

'Yes, thank you!' Jackie's heart gave an extra beat, as if she had plunged into icy water from the deep end.

Everything was being made easy for her to go. Mr. Paul was glad to satisfy such an important client as Veronica Cairgorn. Before she'd 'discovered' his salon his clients had been mostly suburban housewives who wanted a wash and set and an occasional perm. Veronica had introduced an entirely new set from her smart county friends. These women, wealthy and with time on their hands, were always coming in for touching-up or manicures or just 'dressing' for an occasion. They had special shampoos, oil massage, the extras that had almost doubled his income in the last six months. He was thinking how he might open a beauty salon — maybe put Jackie in charge. The smarter women seemed to prefer her to the other girls. Her quiet, refined manner which was always polite but never obsequious, was just right. He'd miss her for those three weeks, but it was worth it to keep Mrs. Cairgorn happy — and a good advertisement, too.

'Well, it's all arranged!' Jackie said to Rona as their first clients came through the door. 'I'll be off on the twentieth of this month.'

'Lucky girl!' Rona had time to say before she went forward with a polite, 'Good afternoon, Madam!'

Jackie waited for some of Rona's excitement on her behalf to infect her but her emotions seemed to remain curiously numb while she waited for the date of departure. With Chris, she could not help a certain restraint which he apparently did not notice. If he did, he must have put it down to tiredness. They went to the cinema, went dancing, had supper and television at her home — it was all automatic and without any special excitement or argument. For once, Chris made no reference to the little black book, and most of their conversation was about Veronica Cairgorn and the kind of 'holiday' they imagined it would be for Jackie. Chris was much more enthusiastic than Jackie, telling her over and over again:

'You'll probably have a wonderful time, darling.'

If only he'd added, 'I wish to God I was coming with you.'

The numbness did not ease even when the huge Comet climbed smoothly into the air. Her parting with Chris was neither difficult nor painful. She had imagined she would feel torn in half when the time came to say goodbye. The ardour of his last kiss at the Airport aroused no answering feelings in her heart.

And her mother, usually so helpless and demanding, said, 'Have a wonderful time, darling, and don't worry about me. I'll manage quite well on my own.'

'Almost as if Mum as well as Chris wants me out of the way!' Jackie thought, realizing she was being child-ish and unreasonable.

The pretty stewardess started to bring round the lunch trays.

Jackie looked at the woman beside her. Veronica was lying back in her chair which the hostess had pushed into a reclining position for her soon after take-off. As usual, Veronica was heavily but perfectly made-up — not a shade too much eye-shadow, the dark thin brows carefully pencilled in where the natural ones had been removed. Her small, usually discontented, mouth was softened in sleep.

'She's not nearly so bad as we all supposed in the salon,' Jackie thought with surprise.

Veronica had gone out of her way to charm her young companion. Instead of using the usual imperial tone of voice Jackie had expected, Veronica spoke in soft, friendly undertones, asking Jackie if she had everything she wanted for the trip. She had bought her magazines and coffee at the Airport and given up the window seat in the plane so that Jackie could have the best view from the giant airliner.

'You must call me Veronica, Jackie. Although you are working for me, I would like us to be friends. I'm quite sure you aren't the type to take advantage of me and I know you'll be tactful. Naturally, I'll expect you to be with me unless I'm with other people- then you'll just make yourself scarce. Now, my dear, tell me more about this fiancé of yours. I can't tell you how pleased I am he decided to let you come.'

Jackie wondered if she could discuss Chris without being or seeming disloyal. Her mother, who'd known him since he'd started at the local grammar school in his first pair of long trousers, could see no wrong in him. Besides, she was far too conventional in a strictly suburban way for Jackie to dream of discussing with her mother the more intimate problems of her relationship with Chris. But Veronica Cairgorn was a woman of the world — experienced, married, travelled. Her opinion would at least be unbiased.

Jackie found herself talking about her problems with only the briefest hesitation. She was met with instant sympathetic understanding.

'My dear, even in 1962 the majority of people won't accept that passion and women — nice women — should be mentioned in the same breath. Sex is still a naughty word and 'nice girls don't have physical needs.' Statistics are quoted proving that half the young female population are taking sex seriously, and then they are classed as Beatniks — Teddy-girls — teenage hooligans. Believe me, Jackie, I'm on your side in this. What beats me is why you haven't told the boyfriend just how you feel.'

Jackie blushed.

'Chris wouldn't understand. In a way, he kind of worships me. I'm his ideal girl — his perfect woman. He puts me on a pedestal and I suppose I don't really want to come off it. I couldn't bear it if he stopped loving me.'

Veronica raised her eyebrows.

'Better make sure now rather than after you are married that he isn't one of those cold types. I'm a firm believer in trial marriages. You've got to have a satisfactory sex life or the marriage is doomed.'

'Just as mine is doomed,' Veronica thought harshly. Unlike this girl, however, *she* had no one but herself to blame. She'd been madly, desperately and passionately in love with a penniless journalist. After five years as his mistress, she'd thrown him over for Carlton Cairgorn — a man of fifty without the least attraction for her. But he was rich — so damn rich she could have anything in the world she wanted! She'd married Cairgorn believing she could go on having Tony, too — but she'd been wrong. Tony had cut her out of his life the way he might have cut out a tumour or a cancer. The love he'd had for her had turned to hate and he despised her for marrying money.

Now Carlton was teetering on the borderline of another heart attack — the next might kill him. Veronica, honest as always with herself, hoped it would. She could no longer go on pretending solicitude or affection for a man she loathed. She knew that her departure for Switzerland when he was still so ill had infuriated and hurt him; knew she risked being cut out of his will. But she'd reached the point where she no longer cared. She wanted some fun and she meant to have it. She had enough put by in the bank to keep her in luxury for years ahead. That much she granted Carlton — he'd been generous enough. And she'd been frugal — spending little of her personal allowance from him and letting him make her presents of jewellery, clothes, the mink, the handsome air-luggage which now was stored away at the back of the plane.

Veronica sighed. This young girl beside her was so frightfully young

— so innocent — so much on the threshold of life. It seemed a hundred years since *she'd* been twenty-one — poor, but full of hope and romantic beliefs.

'Maybe the boyfriend will miss you so much he'll be wild to marry you when you get back!' she told Jackie, smiling. 'You might meet a glamorous, eligible young bachelor, and write glowing letters home about him — make the boyfriend thoroughly jealous.'

It wasn't such a bad idea, Jackie thought, to make Chris jealous. Not that any other man could seriously interest her. Chris was her one and only love — her true love. Since she'd been sixteen and first fallen in love with him, she'd never met a man she liked better.

'I'll always love him, always!' she thought as the hostess came forward with their lunch.

'Ah, champagne!' said Veronica, yawning. 'Let's drink to a happy holiday, Jackie. Here's fun — for us both.'

★　★　★

Jackie saw a rebirth of Veronica's imperious manner when they finally reached the hotel in Crans-sur-Sierre — the resort in Vaud where Veronica had reserved rooms.

It seemed that Jackie's room was on the top floor, whereas Veronica's was on the first.

'But I want my companion on the same floor!' Veronica insisted in a voice which clearly did not anticipate argument.

The anxious receptionist did not understand much English, so Jackie stepped forward and sorted out the muddle in her expert French. Through constant conversation at home with her mother, she'd never forgotten the language of her early childhood.

'Apparently you wrote asking for a room for yourself and your maid. The hotel always put servants on the top floor,' Jackie translated, smiling.

Veronica looked annoyed.

'Well, tell them I insist on a double front room for myself, with balcony and bathroom, and an adjoining single room for you.'

It was finally smoothed out and Jackie was grateful to her employer as she unpacked the smaller of her suitcases in the privacy of the sunny bedroom adjoining Veronica's. It was spacious and very comfortable with french windows onto the balcony and the most fantastic picture-post-card views of the snow-covered mountains across the valley.

'Jackie!' Veronica's voice. She would have to look at everything later. Her job here had begun and work must come before pleasure.

'Oh, Jackie, unpack that big revelation, will you? I want to get into slacks before lunch. Everyone wears ski-clothes here in the day and usually after-ski-slacks at night. You'll find the ice-blue ones at the bottom somewhere.'

By the time Jackie had helped Veronica dress, backcombed her hair and retouched her make-up, it was already half-past-one. She had no time to change from her tweed coat and skirt as she followed Veronica obediently into the dining room. She felt travel-weary and a bit out of her depth in such an expensive and luxurious hotel, but nothing in her cool, calm posture betrayed her.

They were shown to a window table overlooking the magnificent view of the Rhône valley. The sun was so bright on the snow that coloured blinds had been drawn outside, making the room cool and shadowy.

'It's all so beautiful!' Jackie said, staring out of the window, and added, quickly, 'And you look lovely, Veronica. That pale-blue is very becoming with your dark hair and eyes.'

Veronica relaxed, ordering a bottle of *vin-du-pays* from the hovering wine-waiter, and said kindly:

'You look nice too, Jackie. Incidentally, there's a young man at the table over there who can't keep his eyes off you. I suppose you don't have any friends or relations living out here still?'

Jackie turned her head slightly and at once saw the young man Veronica had referred to. There was no mistaking him for he was staring at her openly in a very un-English direct manner. His eyes crinkled and smiled, a teasing, mischievous smile.

She looked away slightly annoyed. She wasn't in the least interested in him — or any young man. Her heart was all too firmly in Chris's keeping.

Veronica looked amused.

'Well, you're off to a good start, Jackie. He looks like a young Apollo. My, how handsome! Have you ever seen anyone so sunbronzed?'

'I really didn't notice,' Jackie said truthfully.

She passed Veronica the basket of bread rolls.

'Madame? Mademoiselle?'

Startled, Jackie looked up to see the young man standing beside their table, his eyes — they were a brilliant sky-blue — still smiling that teasing smile.

'I would like very much to welcome you both to our hotel.'

His English accent was very good but just sufficiently broken to be attractive.

'I hope you will enjoy your stay with us. The snow is excellent if you enjoy the ski?'

'Sure we do!' Veronica answered easily, her eyes sizing up the man now looking at her. He reminded her of someone — who was it? Maybe she'd remember later. He was certainly extremely attractive — perhaps a bit too young for her.

'You will allow me to introduce myself. I am Antoine de Verre. My father owns the hotel.'

'This is Miss Jacqueline Kemster, my name is Cairgorn — Veronica Cairgorn.'

He bowed, Continental fashion, and then politely withdrew.

'But charming!' Veronica said with a smile. 'I'm not so sure I'm going to let you have him, Jackie. He might tempt you to be unfaithful to your Christopher.'

'I don't want him!' Jackie retorted quickly. She was flustered and a little embarrassed. But Veronica just laughed.

'But he wants you, I think. Don't be such a silly girl, Jackie. You don't have to be *serious* about him. Just have some fun. Or are you afraid to trust yourself with him? I'll admit *he* would tempt the hind leg off a donkey. What a naughty boy! Ah, well, we'll see. Now, what are we going to have, Jackie? I'm starving.'

Jackie tried to concentrate on the menu but she couldn't help hearing Antoine de Verre's voice as he talked a little too loudly to the elderly woman beside him.

'*Mais, Maman — c'est la petite qui je trouve ravissante — elle s'appéle Jaqueline. Elle est charmante, n'est-ce-pas?*'

'What is he saying?' Veronica asked wickedly.

Jackie translated.

'Oh, so his companion is his mother,' Veronica commented. 'I suppose he realized we could hear his voice, or perhaps he doesn't know you speak French? Jackie, I do believe you're blushing.'

Jackie was furious with herself and Veronica. She felt young and gauche and wished the incident had never happened to spoil their first meal in this lovely hotel.

Veronica did not require Jackie's company that afternoon and preferred to lie in a deckchair on the sun-terrace, her face covered in sun oil. Jackie decided to go down to the village to see about hiring skis.

She changed into the pale-grey ski-pants which made her legs look longer and slimmer than ever, pulled on a cherry sweater and heavy ski-boots, and left the hotel.

Outside, the warmth of the sun beat down upon her like an electric fire. She put on her dark glasses and drew a deep breath of the frosty, champagne-like air. Her heart was singing with the sheer joy of being alive — of being here — young, full of energy, and halfway up a Swiss mountain with plenty of time free to do anything she wanted.

'Not ski-ing, Mademoiselle Jacqueline?'

It was Antoine de Verre — falling in beside her as if it were the most natural thing in the world to do — as if they were old friends.

'I'm just going to arrange about skis,' she replied coldly. Strangely, she was no longer embarrassed by him. She was quite confident that she could get rid of him as soon as she pleased.

He must be well over six feet tall, she thought, for he towered above her and she was tall — five-feet seven. He, too, wore pale-grey tight-fitting trousers and a brilliant blue ski-sweater that exactly matched his eyes. In the sunlight his bronze colour was remarkable.

'You permit that I should help you?'

'It's not really necessary . . . ' Jackie began and then shrugged her shoulders. After all, why not? There was no harm in letting him accompany her. It was even rather pleasing to have such a handsome escort. There were many feminine heads turning in Antoine's direction as they walked down the ice-packed road to the busy high street.

Antoine shouldered a way through the crowds — most of whom were in ski-clothes — and into a little shop overflowing with skis and boots and batons.

'You've ski'd before?' he asked. 'If so, you will be advised to have the new metal-head skis — they are very good if you fall. They are automatically separated from the boots so you do not break your ankles.'

She was interested in these and gratefully allowed him to arrange everything for her which he did efficiently and knowledgeably. Presently, they were outside in the sunshine again, Antoine carrying the new skis over one shoulder.

'And now?' he asked.

Jackie replied firmly:

'And now we part — I to start on the nursery slopes. I haven't ski'd since I was a little girl and I don't even know if I'll be able to stand up.'

'Then I will accompany you — give you the lesson, no?'

'No!' Jackie retorted, 'I'd rather be on my own if I'm going to take a header into the snow.'

He left without argument and as soon as he was out of sight Jackie fastened on her skis and made off cautiously for the beginners' slopes. At first she was stiff and awkward. Several times she staggered and nearly fell, but gradually she relaxed. Simultaneously her feeling for the sport returned, and with it, miraculously, her balance.

Exhilarated by the progress she was making, she eventually took the ski-lift up to the top and commenced a more direct run down. She tried a Christie-turn and pulled it off. As she did so, Antoine de Verre shot past her, called out 'Bravo!' then disappeared amongst the other skiers in a cloud of fine snow as he twisted and turned in highly expert fashion.

Jackie leant on her batons and watched him with a mixture of admiration and amusement. He was showing-off — but then he could afford to. He was a first-class skier and that alone earned her respect. She realized that he'd probably not been on the nursery slopes in years and was only here this afternoon because of her.

The fact was strangely unsettling. She was flattered and perturbed too. Although Veronica had jokingly suggested that she should find a boyfriend in order to make Chris jealous, she'd had no intention of doing so. Yet now, suddenly, she found herself feeling oddly excited by Antoine's interest in her.

Jackie knew she was attractive. She had a lovely figure and long slender legs which Chris had often told her were quite 'stunning.' Not so long ago her mother had told her she stood a good chance of becoming a model but Jackie had been quite content to leave school at sixteen and start as a junior in a hairdresser's salon. She was not strictly a career-girl. She wasn't even particularly ambitious. Provided she had a satisfactory job, and could earn enough to dress well and pay for her few amusements such as the tennis-club membership and a dramatic society, and help a bit towards the upkeep of the home, she set no great store by money. When Jackie's father died her mother had been left an annuity that kept them both comfortable. It wasn't until Jackie fell in love with Chris that money suddenly became important because it was important to him.

He had ambition enough for them both! Jackie thought wryly. He wanted for her everything he'd missed in his own home — that's why he was so single-minded about buying their own little house and furnishing it before they were married.

'Once we start raising a family, we'll never be able to afford anything,' he had said with serious intensity.

Out here, in the hot sunshine

sparkling on the white snows, their problems all seemed very far away. Jackie realized suddenly that it was a very long time since she had felt the same thrill of excitement that quickened her breathing and made her want to shout or sing aloud from sheer *joie de vivre*. Life hadn't been exciting — it had been dull. Was that why she had wanted something more from Chris? Something more from their lovemaking than boy-and-girl kisses and caresses?

Jackie wondered now if she were more Swiss than English. Because she favoured her mother in looks, their friends had always said she took after her mother. But inside — deep down buried inside her, Jackie knew she was full of a strange fire; capable of big and momentous events if the opportunity to express herself ever came her way; capable of a far greater love than Chris seemed to want from her.

She took a deep breath and in a sudden moment of wild abandon, shoved herself off down the slopes and let her skis carry her down across the snow as fast as they would. She reached the ski-lift hut at the foot of the hill sooner than she expected and was forced into a sudden quick Christie which, surprisingly, again came off perfectly.

'*Magnifique!* Too good for these little mountains. Tomorrow you must come up to Cri d'Err with me!'

It was Antoine again. He must have been waiting at the hut to watch her come down. She felt a little thrill of pure vanity that she should have done so well before his eyes.

'All right! But I warn you, that was a complete fluke!'

They went up together, the ski-lift carrying them to the top in a few minutes. Antoine asked her if she would like to go down once more but she shook her head, laughing.

'I'd probably fall and spoil the good impression!'

He grinned at her understandingly.

'Then tea at Le Sporting Club,' he

said firmly. 'You will like it there, Miss Jacqueline. At five o'clock we dance, *le twist* — lots of twist.'

He seemed to take her acceptance for granted. After a moment's hesitation Jackie found herself giving in to him. After all, she thought, why not.

'But I mustn't be late — Mrs. Cairgorn may wonder where I am.'

Over tea, she explained her role. Antoine listened with great interest.

'Then she is very rich, Mrs. Cairgorn?'

'Fabulously so!' Jackie agreed. 'She is married to an American. I gather he is very ill and may die. I don't think she's in love with him — he's miles older than she is.'

'And she is — how you say it — miles older than you?'

Jackie nodded.

'She makes me feel very young and gauche. I wish I were as sophisticated.'

He leant on his elbows on the table and looked deep into her eyes.

'It is strange — when I see you at the lunch table, I think you are very chic — very sophisticated. Now I know that you are not. You are *très jeune fille* — and yet so beautiful. I do not understand how this can be. No lover?'

Jackie blushed and smiled at the same time.

'Oh, you mean boyfriend. As a matter of fact I'm engaged. Hadn't you noticed?' She lifted her hand and showed him her ring.

'But not *amoureux*?'

She pretended she did not understand the question. Fortunately, at that moment the little three-piece band started up with a crash into the latest twist tune and Antoine rose at once.

'I love to dance — and with you, especially!'

It was impossible to be annoyed with him, Jackie discovered. He was amusing even although he was so much a 'lady's man.' He knew all the right things to say at the right time; just how to make a girl feel she was the only one in the world — and the most attractive.

Jackie didn't trust him but she was entertained and despite herself attracted by him. He danced perfectly, his long legs bending athletically to the twist, his slim hips swaying in perfect rhythm. When the tune changed to a slow fox-trot, he held her a little too close, his cheek against hers, his rather deep masculine voice murmuring the song against her hair.

It was with some reluctance that she tore herself away from the tea-dance at six-thirty.

'I really must go. Veronica will be wondering where I am. I don't want to get the sack my first day here!'

He escorted her back to their hotel, telling her he would wait for her to join him in the bar when she had changed — and she was not to worry about Veronica — he would explain it was his fault.

Veronica was in a good mood and welcomed Jackie with a casual:

'Where on earth have you been? Zip

49

me up, there's a dear. Then you can make-up my face for me. I've had a grand afternoon — met some old friends of mine who are also staying here. We're having drinks together before dinner. I wonder if I should wear my pearls with the black angora? Oh, by the way, Jackie, there's a letter for you. It's on my table over there.'

The letter was from Chris. Jackie completed Veronica's toilette and took the airmail envelope to her own room. The feel of it, crisp, thick and unknown, was disturbing. Oddly enough, it was the first letter she had ever had from Chris. Living within a few miles of each other at home, they'd always communicated by phone if they couldn't actually meet. Would it be a love-letter? She hoped so but doubted it. Chris was not a very eloquent lover — he was a little shy and in a very English way, undemonstrative.

She pulled out the pages covered in Chris's neat handwriting and began to read:

'My Darling,

You have only been out of the country an hour and already I am missing you! I feel as if I'd suddenly lost my right arm. Silly, isn't it, but true all the same. I must have been mad ever to encourage you to go and I just don't know how I'm going to get through the next twenty days without you.

Oh, Jackie, my darling, I wonder if you realise how much I love you? I know I'm not much good at telling you to your face — the fact is you are so stunningly beautiful that, face to face with you, I'm struck dumb. Don't laugh, darling. It's true. I can never quite believe that you are my girl. And why you should love a dull junior bank-clerk like me, I shall never know. You do love me, don't you, Jackie? Once or twice lately I've wondered if you were thinking better of marrying me. There isn't anyone else, is there? If so, you've kept him very well hidden. But that's silly — I know I can trust you absolutely and that you'd tell me if you ever stopped loving me or if you met someone you loved more.

Write me a long letter soon, sweetheart, and tell me what you are doing.

I hope you are having a wonderful time and that the wealthy Mrs. Cairgorn is not proving too much for you. It is pouring with rain here and I wonder if you are in the sunshine — lucky girl.

I love you, darling.

Always and for ever,

Your Chris.'

She held the pages against her breast and closed her eyes. It was almost as if Chris were in the room with her and she felt a deep pulsating need for his physical presence.

A moment later she was at the little writing-table, her pen feverishly covering pages of the hotel note-paper, telling Chris of the hotel, the night they had spent in Geneva, the journey by train and cable car, and how much she missed him. She paused, biting the end of the fountain pen. Should she mention Antoine de Verre? She decided not to. It might upset Chris and besides, there was nothing to tell him. She hadn't approved of Veronica's idea to make him jealous. In any case she had no intention of becoming involved.

She finished her letter with a brief description of the place and covered the remaining half-page with a childish scribble — x x x x x x x.

It was far later than she had intended when she went down to the bar. Antoine de Verre was waiting and rose at once to pull out a bar-stool for her.

'I'm sorry I've been so long. I had a letter to write.'

'No apology is necessary. You look so beautiful, it has been well worth the wait.'

'He's too smooth with his compliments,' Jackie thought critically. Obviously, Antoine had made a study of the art of flirtation. No doubt living in the hotel as he did, he spent his time attracting and being attracted by unattended female visitors. But it was impossible to be irritated by him for long. However deliberate, his technique was very effective.

'I have asked the permission of Mrs. Cairgorn that you should dine with me. And after dinner we will go to the Whisky Go-Go. This I think you will enjoy — lots of dancing and a lovely log-fire and candles. *Très romantique!*'

'I'll bet,' Jackie thought, but decided there was no real reason why she should not fall in with his plans. Loving Chris so much, she was immune to Antoine's charms. A friendship was one thing but it would have to stay platonic.

She was a little disconcerted and put off her guard when much later Antoine agreed with her.

'We will at all times remember the fiancé', he said, as they danced cheek to cheek in the smoky half-light of the night club to a sentimental slow fox-trot. 'Because of this Christopher, I will not tell you I am a little in love with you. I will do like this and kiss your cheek. We will be no more than friends, close, close friends.'

Jackie pulled away from his embrace and walked off the dance floor. She was angry with him and with herself. It was so silly to have imagined one could be friends with a young man like Antoine de Verre. He was typically French and she ought to have known better than to suppose he wouldn't try to make love to her. The worst of it was, she'd let him succeed — at least to the point of arousing in her a sentimental dreaminess.

'NO!' she told herself, sharply. 'It's more than that!' She was thoroughly aroused; her arms bare in the sleeveless evening jersey top, tingling to the touch of his hands; her heart thudding at the sound of that soft voice against her ear. Many of the couples were clasped close against one another, arms entwined, bodies pressed close, and that's how she wanted to dance with Antoine.

Even when they danced the quicker, noisier number like the twist, there was an answering sparkle in her eyes, a heady excitement that was born of her consciousness of his consciousness of her as a woman. Instead of trying not to attract him she had been as provocative in her movements as any other girl on the floor.

She felt cheap and resentful — it was almost as if her behaviour was a physical act of infidelity to Chris. She wanted Antoine's touch, his nearness — yes, his kisses — and she ought not to let any man but Chris arouse her in this way.

'I want to go home!' she said, childishly.

He looked at her long and intently and then rose and said simply:

'I will pay the bill. You fetch your coat.'

Now she hesitated. To walk back to the hotel in the brilliant, dazzling moonlight no longer seemed a way of escape, with Antoine beside her . . .

'I won't let him kiss me. I'll say 'no' if he asks,' she promised herself.

But he didn't ask. He just pulled her into his arms and bending his head, pressed his lips hard against her own.

★ ★ ★

Her resistance lasted only a second and then she was returning the kiss — never wanting it to stop. It didn't matter that this man was a stranger — he didn't seem like one — the touch of his mouth, his hands, his body — all were familiar and known to her in some strange predestined way. If she thought at all, it was only that she couldn't help herself — this had had to happen. In a way, the arms now caressing her shivering body were Chris's arms but, unlike Chris, this man did not break away from their embrace. His body was as much on fire as her own — he wanted her as much as she wanted him.

'No!' she cried violently. 'No!'

For a moment she had to struggle

against his male strength but then quite suddenly his arms dropped to his sides and they stood in silence, breathing deeply, wordless in a lost world.

'Please — I'm sorry. Take me back to the hotel — I'm sorry!' The words were whispered, but he heard.

The taut lines of his face relaxed and he smiled.

'But of course, *chérie*. It is late. Tomorrow is another day, no? And I shall take you up to Cri d'Err.'

'No, I can't come — I can't ski well enough,' Jackie said frantically. 'Another day, perhaps, when I've had more practice.'

He stood looking at her, a smile on his lips, but not in his eyes. For a few moments, Jackie knew fear. The handsome face held a curious expression — almost cruel.

'You must not be afraid of me, Jacqueline. I am no wolf in sheep's clothing. See, you are trembling *ma petite*.'

She pulled her hands away, furious that they should have betrayed her, and confused by her lack of composure. It was totally unlike her to be uncertain of herself — to behave like a gauche schoolgirl. How silly he must think her!

'I'm not in the least afraid of you, Antoine,' she said quickly, and with dignity. 'I just want to go home — to the hotel, I mean. I'm tired and cold.'

His expression changed again. He was now all solicitude. Somehow she managed to thank him politely for the pleasant evening and, as quickly as possible, left him to go upstairs to her room. Once there, she flung herself on the bed, her breathing uneven, her whole body filled with a sense of escape from danger.

For several minutes she lay still, then sat up, shaking her head as if to clear her mind.

How silly this was. The heady mountain air was playing tricks with her mental equilibrium. It was absurd to let Antoine de Verre affect her in this way — in so many ways. In one short evening, she reflected ruefully, she had run the gamut of emotions and that did not exclude fear.

She felt uncomfortably ashamed. Chris would be horrified — he simply wouldn't believe she could be so silly — and with a man who was still virtually a stranger.

'I shan't go with him tomorrow!' she told herself firmly. 'The less I see of him from now on, the happier I'll be.' It wasn't even as if she really liked him.

But she had underestimated Antoine de Verre. She could not have known that the word denial was not in his vocabulary. The only son of adoring parents, he had been completely spoiled as a child, his every whim indulged. As a young man, his exceptional good looks and athletic ability made him instantly attractive to girls and women. He soon learned the right ways to treat each of them if he was to achieve his own ends. He mastered the techniques of flirtation and conquest with the same wholehearted attention that he mastered an athletic sport.

Jacqueline, with her curious combination of elegant sophistication and virginal innocence, attracted and intrigued him. He had sensed the passion lurking beneath the cool exterior and was excited by the challenge she unwittingly offered. The unknown fiancé did not bother him — he merely increased the challenge. Antoine never doubted that with a little time, patience and ingenuity, he would ultimately succeed.

3

Jackie sat opposite Antoine in the cable-car taking them up to Cri d'Err, her eyes studiously avoiding his teasing face. She felt irritable and cornered. Somehow, Antoine had persuaded Veronica that *she* would enjoy the run down from Cri d'Err, and that Jackie must accompany them. Consequently, Veronica had refused to listen to Jackie's excuses.

'Antoine told me himself you were quite up to the standard of ski-ing necessary. Now don't be such a silly girl, Jackie. I *want* you to come.'

After that, she couldn't very well refuse.

Apart from gazing at Jackie from time to time with that mischievous small-boy smile, Antoine gave all his attention to Veronica — who seemed flattered and amused.

'If he thinks he'll make me jealous,

he's mistaken!' Jackie thought, and gave her own attention to the glorious view from the cable-car terminus on top of the mountain. The sun was shining from a flawless blue sky and all around them skiers were laughing and enjoying themselves on snow which, though soft, was still excellent for ski-ing.

Without waiting for Antoine or Veronica, Jackie fastened on her skis and propelled herself off the first leg of the run down. Not knowing the terrain, she should have let Antoine lead her down the first time, but she didn't care. If she was going to fall — then she would fall; better that than letting Antoine think she was dependent on him as a guide.

He passed her halfway down and was nearly the cause of her first fall. She just managed to stop unsteadily and watched him shoot away from her with his easy grace — the beautiful, relaxed movements of a ballet-dancer, she thought, admiringly. Despite her irritation, she could not help being impressed. To see those fascinating fluid movements of the legs, the skis seeming almost to glide above the surface of the snow rather than on it, was a revelation.

Veronica drew up to a halt beside her and said, breathlessly:

'Great heavens, can that boy ski! How are you doing Jackie? I'm fearfully out of practice.'

They both nevertheless managed to reach the halfway mark without a bad fall. They decided to go back to the top and not complete the full run through the woods until the afternoon.

'Antoine has organized lunch at the hut on top. He'll meet us there,' Veronica said as they paid for their ski-lift tickets and joined the queue waiting to go back up the mountain.

Jackie relaxed, feeling the tautened nerves unwind as she lay back in a deck chair on the terrace outside the hut, the sun burning her face which, like the other skiers, she had covered in oil. The only make-up they wore was lipstick and mascara. Even Antoine's arrival could not shake her out of the lazy, contented apathy the hot sun and glittering snow induced.

But by the time they had finished lunch, the sky had clouded and skiers were beginning to move off in numbers.

Antoine looked at the sky and the mist now rolling in up the valley.

'Soon it will not be nice, we must go down,' he said, seriously. 'You two first, I will follow. In a mountain mist it is easy to become lost if you do not know your way very well.'

Veronica, however, refused to be hurried. By the time she had put on her dark blue pullover and white anorak, fixed her hair and face and had a last cup of coffee, the air was several degrees colder. Jackie shivered, feeling the icy chill of the misty fog creeping towards them.

'Hurry, please, Mrs. Cairgorn!' Antoine said several times. 'Maybe it is best you two to go down by cable-car.'

But Veronica would not hear of it.

'I'm not missing the run down for

any old fog. It's all very well for you, Antoine — you had two runs down already.'

'Very well, but please hurry!'

They were the last skiers to go.

Perhaps because they were cold and a little stiff from the unaccustomed exercise, Veronica and Jackie both fell several times. Jackie, on her third fall, wrenched a muscle in her leg which slowed her up. Antoine looked at her and the thickening fog in obvious concern.

'You go on, Mrs. Cairgorn. Follow that couple over there. I will take care of Jacqueline.'

Jackie realized that the situation was now becoming serious. Something in Antoine's voice convinced her, although he kept telling her she must not worry.

'It is not good for you to ski with the stiff body. Relax. Take your time.'

By the time they had reached the wood, the mist was all around them and it was so dark Jackie found it hard to believe her watch was going when she saw it was not long past three o'clock. The pain in her leg worsened and there was no pleasure at all in the ski-ing. It had become an endurance test.

Experienced as he was, Antoine guessed how she was feeling and on the next bend when she drew up, he looked at her white face and said:

'Maybe it is best not to try further. There is a small hut one kilometre beyond. If you can make it there, we can be safe.'

'No, I'd rather get back to the hotel,' Jackie said shakily. She had begun to feel slightly sick. 'Veronica will worry.'

'My mother will know we are both safe. Ever since I was a small boy I have been on these mountains. She will tell Mrs. Cairgorn of the hut. It is not the first time I have sheltered there.'

Jackie was forced to give in. The remaining kilometre was sheer agony and she did not demur when Antoine took off his skis outside the hut and having removed hers, assisted her inside.

There were two grey army blankets

— damp but at least offering some warmth. Antoine wrapped her in these and set about lighting the paraffin lamp and then the log fire. He seemed quite calm and was, as usual, very efficient.

It was little more than a log cabin but once the lamp was lit and the fire blazing, it seemed a haven to Jackie.

'Now — we will have a drink — then a meal.' Antoine said cheerfully. He had already looked at her leg, skilfully examining the muscles, and said there was little to be done except rest it.

He disappeared outside into the thick fog for a moment or two and came back with a kettle full of snow which he hung on a primitive hook over the log fire. While it was coming to the boil, he searched in a cupboard in one corner of the room and gave a little cry of satisfaction.

'Good — plenty of tinned food. I think we will commence with Ravioli, then follow with venison and petit-pois. After this, we will eat tinned strawberries and cream. How is that for Madame?'

For the first time in several hours, Jackie relaxed and smiled. In a way, this was rather fun. They were safe, warm and had plenty to eat — strong tinned coffee to drink. Antoine was the perfect host, making fun of the makeshift meal and laughing and talking gaily all the while.

Supper over, he sat down cross-legged in front of the fire and brought out a mouth organ from his anorak pocket.

'I will now entertain you with a selection of popular songs of your choice. Yours to command Mademoiselle Jackie!'

He played very well — at first parodying the latest pop songs but drifting into a different mood and playing the more sentimental arias from the light operas. Jackie felt drowsy, warmed by the heat, her mood responding to the witchery of the music. Antoine's face was alight with dancing shadows from the fire. He was in profile and for a moment or two she studied the sculptured lines of his face and jaw until he turned and saw her staring.

He put down his mouth organ and moved over beside her. Guessing her thoughts, he grinned and said:

'I have no intention of taking advantage of the situation. You need have no fear of me, Jackie. I will do nothing which you do not desire.'

Lying there, looking up at him, Jackie knew that it was not the man but herself she had to fear. She believed that he would not force her — even to a kiss — if she did not wish it. *But she did wish it.* She wanted to feel again that same heady excitement she had felt in his arms when they had danced together. She wanted him to kiss her — to go on kissing her . . .

'You know that I am already a little in love with you, my dear little English Miss. Tell me that you like me, too?'

'I don't think I do like you very much!' The words were out before she could stop them. He just laughed.

'But?' he prompted her.

'But you are very attractive — and what's more you know it.'

Again he laughed, a deep-throated chuckle that was completely male.

'Other women have said so — but it is not other women in whom I am interested. It is you, Jackie, with your big, innocent grey eyes and your mouth . . . even in repose your mouth promises so much. Will you keep the promise of your lips? Kiss me, darling — *mon amour!*'

'This is mad — crazy — utterly unreal!' Jackie thought. 'I must be firm — make him understand once and for all that I don't want him . . . '

But already it was too late. His mouth was upon hers and his hands, surprisingly gentle, were cupping her bare shoulders beneath the ski-sweater. She raised her own, meaning to pull his hands away but instead, as if they had a life and will of their own, they merely covered his and pressed them closer.

'I won't let this go too far — just for a moment . . . '

Then suddenly her eyes opened and she saw the little smile of triumph on Antoine's face.

She sat up, pushing his hands away from her body and said desperately:

'No! Leave me alone, Antoine.'

The smile left his face and was replaced by one of cold anger and surprise. He looked at her trembling mouth and said coldly:

'Why? Give me one good reason why I should.'

Her voice was desperate. She held out her hands in helpless appeal.

'Because you promised. You gave me your word. Please, I beg of you, Antoine, leave me alone.'

For a few moments he continued to stare at her, on his face an expression that was both angry and sulky.

'You are tormenting me, Jackie. It is not fair.'

She sat up, straightening her clothes and said:

'I'm sorry, Antoine. I did not fall and hurt my ankle on purpose. It was your idea to come here — not mine. I am not trying to 'tease' you. I thought I had made it absolutely clear that I am in love with another man and that I don't want . . . anything from you.'

Antoine, too, stood up but now a smile played at the corners of his mouth.

'This is not true, Jacqueline. You *do* want me — I know it.'

The colour flared into her cheeks. To hide her face from him, she threw another log onto the fire.

'All right, I'll admit that I find you attractive in a purely physical way. But I don't intend to give way to what I know to be a basic appetite. It may seem strange to you, Antoine, but I never have let a man make love to me and I don't intend to — not until I marry Chris.'

Antoine sat down beside her and now his face was warm and tender again, as he sought to persuade her with words.

'This is the very old-fashioned idea, Jackie. I have known many English girls who have come to our hotel who do not have these out-of-date notions.'

'Perhaps it is old-fashioned. I don't know and I don't care. I don't care either what other English girls do. I don't want anyone but Chris to love me . . . that's all there is to it.'

'He need never know!' Antoine said softly. 'And you have nothing to fear — I would take care of you. What harm can it do?'

Jackie's mouth tightened.

'Why can't you understand! I'm not afraid of any consequences. It isn't that. I'd feel horrible — as if I'd cheated my fiancé. He loves me and he trusts me — and I love him.'

Antoine shrugged his shoulders in a very Continental fashion.

'This great love — it does not seem to me so very big. He lets you come out here alone — a young, beautiful girl. Is he crazy, this *Christophe*, to allow such a thing? Is he so much in love that he can permit you to be away from him for three weeks? When I am in love, I wish all the time to be near, very near, my girl.'

Jackie was silent. Antoine had touched a chord very near her heart. Hadn't she, too, doubted the force of Chris's love when he had actually persuaded her to leave him, rather than tried to keep her at home. But that, she argued again, was only his unselfishness. He hadn't wanted to spoil her chance of a holiday . . .

Even so, she would willingly have forgone this trip if he had asked her to; if he had said:

'I can't bear the thought of three weeks' separation. Stay here, Jackie — let's get married right away . . . '

'So?' Antoine persisted. 'You agree with me?'

'No!' Jackie lied. 'No!' But only because she was afraid to admit to her own fears that Antoine might be right.

Antoine did not press his advantage. He could wait. Already he sensed that Jackie's will was weakening.

He said:

'I am making some more coffee now. You would like it, yes?'

For a little while, he was the perfect amusing companion, telling her stories about gay parties they had had in the summer months, walking up the mountain road with a crowd of boys and girls, eating picnic lunches outside this same hut in the hot sunshine. In the afternoon, they would go to a lake where the water was ice-cold still, and swim. Later, they would come back to the hut and build a camp fire and sing to Antoine's accordion.

'It sounds wonderful fun!' Jackie said, remembering her own childhood in the London suburbs where such excitements could never happen. In retrospect, her childhood seemed very narrow, very restricted. The only excitement she had known was the annual fortnight's holiday at Westcliff-on-Sea; always the same hotel; always the same beach; even the same bedrooms.

'You should come here in the summer,' Antoine said. 'It is very beautiful with the wild flowers and the mountain streams and such warm weather. No fogs or winds or rain as you have in England.'

He leant towards her and put his arm round her shoulders so casually that she could not really object.

'The ankle?' he asked. 'It is paining you?'

She shook her head.

'Only a very little!'

He went outside and came back a moment later with his handkerchief ice cold from the snow. He wrapped it round her leg and in a few minutes the pain had gone.

'Thank you,' she said gratefully. 'I'm sorry to be so helpless.'

Antoine sat down once more beside her and eased their positions so that she was resting her head and back against him.

'More comfortable for you like this!' he said, touching his lips to the fragrance of her hair.

He felt her stiffen slightly and knew that she was conscious of the physical nearness of him. He smiled.

'I think your fiancé cannot object to a goodnight kiss. That would be very silly.'

'I know, but . . . '

He stilled her voice with the hard, sudden pressure of his mouth on hers.

At once, her body caught fire. As always, she struggled against her temptation to surrender but as his hands began to move expertly over her body, she felt herself weakening to the mounting excitement.

'You promise . . . ?' she asked, fighting to free herself.

'Yes, I promise!' Antoine said, understanding her. 'We will not cross the last barrier. Not unless you say 'yes'.'

'I will never do that — never!' she vowed.

But in the morning, as he helped her to move slowly and painfully down the hill to the hotel, she knew that though they had not crossed what Antoine called 'the last barrier,' they might as well have done so. To spend one whole night lying naked in the arms of a man, was hardly less forgivable than to have given herself to him in complete surrender. She felt terribly ashamed.

★　★　★

Jackie knew herself for a coward. She sat on the terrace in the hot sunshine, her face upturned to the brilliant blue of the sky, her eyes closed. She ought to be happy but somehow she was not.

'You're a fool!' Veronica had said several times. 'You won't always be young and attractive, Jackie. Why not make the most of it? Antoine's a very charming young man.'

Veronica seemed determined not to understand that Jackie's principles forbade her to take what Antoine was offering; determined to disregard the fact that she was engaged to Chris and would one day be his wife.

'But you're not yet!' Veronica commented dryly. 'What you do before marriage is your affair. I'm surprised at you, Jackie. Most young girls nowadays . . . '

Jackie asked herself for the hundredth time if she was being a fool. The mind said no but her body, ever treacherous, said yes, yes, yes! But she was afraid. Afraid of committing herself so irrevocably; afraid she would hate herself if she did; afraid to write to Chris and tell him anything about her accident or the night on the mountain with Antoine in case he read between the lines and realized how terribly tempted she had been. For the past week, she had written him nothing but postcards, always non-committal, never mentioning Antoine by name.

'If only Antoine had been thoroughly nasty,' she thought with a feeling of helplessness. He could so easily have broken his promise and made love to her. He had known exactly how near to the point of surrender she had been. But he hadn't taken advantage of her weakness then any more than he had given up trying since!

A faint smile stole across Jackie's cheeks, now tanned a golden brown by the sun. No girl could ever have had a more persistent or attentive admirer. It had been useless for her to try to persuade him that she wouldn't change her mind. He said in his soft teasing way that there was no law against trying to make a girl fall in love; that patience was rewarded; that in any case he enjoyed being with her. Although the injury to her ankle had made any further ski-ing or dancing impossible, she had been to the Sporting Club with him in the afternoons, dined with him, gone for walks in the village and across the golf course, now covered with virgin snow and almost deserted. He had taken her down to the valley in the cable car, given her lunch and taken her round the shops to buy presents for her mother and Rona.

Deep down inside, Jackie knew that she wasn't in love with Antoine. Her love for Chris was too deep-rooted, of too long standing. She could not think seriously, even for a moment, of writing to Chris to ask him to end their engagement. At the same time, Antoine's attraction for her was a constant nagging worry. She might have written it off as mere physical infatuation but his willingness not to force the issue and to remain patient and adoring at her side confused her. He was such a good companion! His continual compliments were flattering even if she sometimes felt they were not altogether genuine. Try as she might, she could not help but like him.

Marriage was never mentioned between them. A hundred times a day, Antoine professed his love for her, but neither of them were deceived as to what he really wanted — not marriage but a love affair.

For hours at night, Jackie had lain awake, asking herself if it were really so wrong? Other girls had experience before marriage. Chris would never know — need never be told. Antoine had told her again and again that she had nothing to fear. She wanted to give way and yet when morning came, her weakness of the night was gone. A letter from Chris or a card from Rona or her mother brought back her ordinary everyday way of life and the principles by which she had so far lived. By afternoon she was weakening again under the pressure of Antoine's words, his gentle almost casual touch; his soft caressing voice.

Last night she allowed him to drive her a little way up the mountain road where they sat alone in his car in the moonlight. Before long, she was in his arms and he was kissing and caressing her. The moonlight, white and pure, had seemed to lend a veil of purity to what Veronica described this morning as a 'glorified necking session.' How horrible it sounded! Yet Jackie realized that was how other people would think of it: how *Chris* would think of it. At the time it had all seemed so romantic; almost inevitable. Chris had been completely forgotten in the tumult of longing to give way to the demands of her bodily senses. She now trusted Antoine not to take advantage of her, she had felt free to return his kisses. Passion, naked and uncontrolled, had flared between them, as it had before in the ski-hut. Fortunately a passing ski-guide, imagining them to be snow-bound, had stopped to enquire if they needed help with the car. Antoine had been furiously and, for a moment, frighteningly angry, but Jackie had looked on the interruption as a kindly Fate stepping in in time to save her from degradation and disaster.

In the handbag at her side lay a long letter to Chris; a letter of confession. Writing it had not only eased her conscience but the fact that she was no longer deceiving Chris acted as a kind of safeguard. Now she had told him about Antoine, she could let the affair continue; certainly she could never do as Antoine wished and for the moment all desire to do so had vanished. She was Chris's girl and when she faced him on the first night of their honeymoon, it should not be with secret shame and the knowledge that she had cheated him. But the letter was still not posted. She had pushed it into her handbag and come out on to the terrace where she could be alone to think about it a little longer. The trouble was, she hadn't, after all, told Chris the whole truth. She had made light of Antoine's compelling attraction for her, mentioned in the most casual way that she had allowed him to kiss her good night.

This was hopelessly far from the truth. She had again last night permitted Antoine to touch and hold her body beneath her thin evening sweater; their kisses, caresses, had been anything but casual. The truth was she had gone very much further with Antoine than she had ever done with Chris.

Perhaps if Chris had been less protective — as violently demanding and passionate as Antoine, she would have been as sorely tempted to enjoy the full delights of marriage before their wedding. But Chris was always so controlled, so careful to keep control of himself.

Jackie could not understand now how she could both respect him for this control and hate him for it at the same time. Considering it now, it seemed almost an insult to her womanhood. Maybe Chris did not find her so unbearably attractive as Antoine! Perhaps he was not as susceptible — as tempted. Such thoughts made her angry with him and hurt and yet, deep down, she knew that Chris was right. To go so far as she had with Antoine last night was playing with fire. It could not stop there for long. Either the fire must burst into its true flare or be put out completely.

It was recognition of this danger that had prompted her to write to Chris. She *must* put an end to these hours alone with Antoine! Now she must try to get their friendship on to purely platonic grounds or stop being alone with him. Otherwise she would never be able to face Chris when she went home.

Veronica did not make things any easier. She had no morals. Jackie had begun to dislike her employer even while she was forced to admit the older woman was generous and, on the whole, good-natured. Her job as a companion had become virtually unnecessary since Veronica had found a 'boy friend.' Except for doing Veronica's hair every evening before dinner, Jackie might as well not be employed. Yet Veronica never spoke of sending her home or mentioned the expense she was incurring by keeping Jackie with her. For this Jackie was grateful but she felt uneasy — even unhappy, knowing that Veronica entertained her friend every night in her bedroom. The man was married, and it was doubly wrong by virtue of the fact Veronica's own husband was very ill at home.

'I won't be like her, I won't!' Jackie vowed. Yet she knew that the moment she was alone once more with Antoine her emotions would overcome her principles in the end.

Perhaps if Veronica had needed her as a companion, it would have been easier to resist Antoine. As it was, Jackie was free all day and every evening, and she knew no one else in the hotel since the older woman did not introduce her to her own circle of friends. But for Antoine, Jackie would have had a very dull and lonely time. And since they both lived in the hotel it was quite impossible for her to refuse to see him again. That was the only answer. She knew it, but could see no way round the problem.

She reached down to her handbag and took out the letter. As she read her own words, she felt her cheeks burning.

'It doesn't mean anything, really, Chris, except that I am missing you terribly. It is really you I want to be kissing, not Antoine. Can you understand this? I know I should feel terribly jealous if I thought you were taking out some other girl but I would trust you as you must trust me . . .'

She dropped the page on her lap with a little cry of self-disgust. How could she expect Chris to trust her when she couldn't trust herself. If he knew what she had really felt — how near she had been to giving way . . .

'Oh, Chris!' she whispered helplessly.

He's a very good skier and a good dancer, too, and Veronica seems to think he's a carbon copy of Flint — you know, the cowboy on T.V. But he isn't really my type and there is absolutely no question of my being in love with him . . .

That last at least was true. She couldn't be in love with Antoine, since her whole heart belonged to Chris and she would never, never wish to be married to anyone else.

I suppose it's just the normal reaction when lonely girl meets lonely boy. I wouldn't have written about it at all except that I don't want us ever to have any secrets from each other . . .

That was a lie, too. The half-truths she had written concealed the real truth — the truth that she was desperately attracted to Antoine and that if she were less of a coward she would have given way days ago. What she really feared was the feeling she might have afterwards — of hating herself, of having cheapened herself and the love she shared with Chris, of regretting something she could never undo. It wasn't just love for Chris which was creating the last barrier — it was her fear of the consequences.

Suddenly, angrily, she tore the pages in half and screwed them into a ball. What good, after all, did this letter do? she thought bitterly. It changed nothing and would only hurt and worry Chris. When she got home she would tell him, explain everything. In another week she would be home and this would all seem unreal, like a tormenting dream. She would be able to see herself and Antoine in their proper perspective, and there would be no need for lies or half-truths.

'Darling! *Mon amour.*'

She felt a light kiss on her forehead and the colour rushed into her cheeks as she raised her head to see Antoine smiling down at her.

'Don't,' she said quickly, anxiously. 'Someone might see!'

Antoine's blue eyes grinned down at her. Then he took her hand and sat beside her, saying lazily:

'And so? All the world must know by now that I am crazy about my proper little English Miss. Ah, Jackie, how sweet you look lying there like a little kitten in the sunshine. I wish we were alone — quite alone. How is your poor ankle? Do you think you might be able to have one little dance tonight?'

The blush faded from Jackie's cheeks and she said quickly:

'I'm not going out anywhere with you tonight, Antoine.'

'Ah, then we will stay in the hotel and talk!'

'You don't understand!' Jackie said. 'I was trying to tell you that . . . that I want to be alone.'

She felt stupid, more especially as Antoine seemed bent on misinterpreting her words.

'Then you are not well? Something is wrong?'

'I'm quite well! Nothing is wrong. I . . . Antoine this is all so silly — so hopeless . . . our being together, I mean. I know that each time you take me out you hope that . . . that I'll do as you wish. But I won't . . . ' Her voice was rising and she checked it quickly and almost whispered: 'I'm in love with my fiancé. I'll never do anything to hurt him.'

Antoine's smile faded and for an instant he looked angry. Then he smiled and said gently, persuasively:

'But we have talked of all this before. I have given you my word that nothing shall happen that you do not yourself want. You tell me now you wish to be alone. Is this because you are afraid I will break my word?'

'No . . . no! You know I trust you.'

'Then it is yourself you do not trust?'

Her silence was his answer and he laid his hand gently on the back of her shining head.

'You must not be afraid to live, my little one. You have a saying in your country, I believe — that when one is very old it is not the things one has done one regrets, but those one has not done. Won't you be a little sad, Jackie, remembering your brief holiday in my country and the young man who loved you so much? Won't you regret just a little that you will have gone home never knowing what fulfilment could be?'

'I don't want to know!' Jackie said violently, but even as she spoke she knew it wasn't true. Antoine was probably right — she would always remember and wonder . . .

'I'm utterly inconsistent!' she told herself. 'One moment I'm sure that any relationship with Antoine is wrong, yet the next moment he makes me feel that I'm being prudish and afraid of life

'— and love . . . '

'Why can't you leave me alone? I'm in love with Chris! I don't want you to touch me!'

But her hand would not obey her will and lay trembling, burning beneath his own.

Antoine said nothing. Her hand answered him more truthfully than her voice. There was still another week before she went home — a whole week, and although he had had to wait far longer than he had anticipated, he would savour his final victory all the more.

Veronica came out on to the terrace, her ski-boots glistening with melting snow, her eyes gay and amused.

'How are the two love-birds? My, but you've caught the sun, Jackie — or has Antoine just said something to make you blush?'

'She's horrible — horrible!' Jackie thought, and getting up as quickly as she could, she hurried away from them, up to her room, leaving them staring after her in surprise.

4

Antoine looked down at Jackie with his peculiarly charming smile. It was half-teasing, half-ardent, and Jackie was never quite proof against it. He made her feel young and *gauche* and at the same time all woman.

'You cannot be afraid to come ski-ing with me!' he taunted her. 'Look up there to the mountain — see how the sunshine has brought everyone onto the slopes. You will have a thousand chaperones, *ma petite*!'

Jackie hesitated. It seemed so stupid to refuse. The hotel doctor had pronounced the sprain quite better and told her that she could ski again if she wished. She had not told Veronica because she did not wish Antoine to know. But he had found out all the same, and as she had guessed, he had at once tried to make her join him.

'I doubt if I could tackle anything more than the nursery slopes,' she said, but her voice gave her away — it was too hesitant.

'I will look after you. We will take the run down very gently, in stages. First, I think, we will order lunch to eat up at Cri d'Err.'

He had already taken matters out of her hands, and in half-an-hour they were in the tiny cable car swinging over the tops of the fir trees, watching the valley drop far below them as they swayed gently upwards towards the mountain top.

Jackie relaxed. She felt at once a surge of excitement as her mind pulled a curtain firmly across any more qualms of conscience. It was impossible not to enjoy the brilliant sparkling glisten of virgin snow in the hot sunshine; impossible not to feel a thrill of adventure as the ski-run itself came into view below them and she could see the skiers twisting and turning so swiftly and gracefully in their descent.

A few weeks ago she would not have believed it possible for anyone to be bitten by the ski-bug against their will. Yet here she was, longing to fasten on the skis Antoine had stacked on the front of the cable car, eagerly awaiting the moment when he would turn his head over his shoulder, skis and batons poised ready, to say, 'We're off!'

But first they joined the laughing crowd of young people on the terrace outside the hut at the cable car terminus. Antoine went in to the busy bar to fetch beer for himself and coffee for Jackie, while she leaned back against the wall of the hut, her face upturned to the hot sunshine. She was reminded suddenly of her last visit to this place — the day when the mountain mist had descended so frighteningly and caught Antoine and herself in its swift path. She gave a quick anxious glance at the cloudless blue sky and then smiled. One couldn't, she told herself firmly, go through life afraid of everything. She was here to enjoy herself and nothing was going to spoil the day's perfection.

Antoine, too, was in the same carefree mood. Jackie's company added the necessary aura of excitement to the day. He was an excellent and enthusiastic skier, but the novelty of the sport was not in itself quite enough. Jackie's presence made all the difference. Presently he would start off ahead of her, showing off his proficiency and ski-ing all the better for the knowledge that she was watching and admiring him. Then he would pause while she came down more slowly, calling out words of advice and encouragement.

'This is fun, no?' he said, smiling, as they finished the last remnants of the packed lunch they had brought with them.

Jackie sighed.

'It's perfect!' she said, stretching her arms above her head. 'What I find so hard to understand is how it can be so warm with all this snow.'

'You should be here in March!' Antoine told her. 'Then I ski just in trousers and one's back is burnt black with the sun.'

'In England, when we have snow it is cold, damp and depressing,' Jackie said. For a moment her mind lingered over the terrible weeks of snow and ice following on Christmas, 1962 — the struggle to get to work, to keep warm indoors, let alone out in the icy East winds.

'We have the perfect climate!' Antoine remarked. He leant over and placed his hand lightly over hers. 'You should marry me and live here always. You have no idea how much healthier you look since you arrived here. You looked so pale and thin. Now you are brown and the shadows have gone from beneath your eyes. Tell me, Jackie, do you work very hard at home? You have long hours doing the *coiffeurs* of rich ladies like Veronique?'

'It's not too bad — I enjoy my work!' Jackie said loyally, although at this moment the thought of the salon was almost unbearable.

'Marry me and stay here always!' Antoine said again.

Jackie was not sure if he was serious. She looked shyly at his face and saw that he was smiling.

'You do not believe that I wish to marry you?'

The question hung between them. Antoine himself did not know the answer. He had not intended the question seriously, but now that he considered the idea it did not seem so bad. Jackie would be very useful in the hotel — she was attractive to look at, and she had a quiet, simple, very English charm which he knew would appeal to their visitors. One day his father would retire and he would be the owner. Then he would have to marry in order to have a wife to do all that his mother did now.

But the inevitability of his future depressed Antoine even as he considered it. It was not what he wanted — to waste his life being servile to a lot of rich people. He wanted to be rich himself — to travel round the world at will, exploring, discovering new interests, to satisfy his ever present need for excitement. It would not do to saddle himself with a wife and thereby curtail his activities.

To his relief Jackie said quietly:

'You know I am already engaged to Chris.'

'*Quel dommage!*' Antoine said. 'It is indeed a great pity there is always this Christopher to haunt us.'

Jackie stood up. She didn't want to think about Chris now. Nor did she wish the mood of the day to become serious. But even as Antoine moved away to collect their skis her eyes followed him with curiosity. Had he been serious? Was he really in love with her?

But there was no more time for thought. All her concentration was needed for the difficult first part of the run. Antoine went ahead, moving effortlessly, more like a skater than a skier, she thought. He was nearly upright, his body moving only slightly with the turn of his hips as he swung in perfect Christie turns to right or left. He was like a slim, graceful bird.

At first her muscles ached from the unaccustomed strain, but after five minutes the tension of fear left her and she began to move less stiffly and therefore to ski much better.

'That was fine, fine!' Antoine congratulated her as they reached the beginning of the next part of the descent. Here was the terminal of another ski-lift, a kind of halfway to the top stop.

'If you are not too tired,' Antoine suggested, 'let's go down here, rest a few moments and then come back. I think this is the best part of the run.'

He looked into Jackie's glowing, excited face and felt his heart thump with a purely physical response. If he could only make love to her now. He knew very well how she was feeling — almost intoxicated with hot sun, with the cold rush of champagne-like air on her cheeks, and the thrill of achievement in bringing off a good turn. At this moment she would not say 'no.'

He bent suddenly and kissed her full on the lips. Jackie laughed up at him, surprised but too happy to be angry. He had judged her emotional state exactly.

During the second run down Antoine followed close beside her.

'Don't worry about me — I won't let you knock me over!' he reassured her.

She heard his voice calling instructions —

'Bend the knee a little — turn here after me — straight now over the next hump — now to the left, to the right — relax . . .'

Doing as he said, her ski-ing seemed to improve fantastically. Now they were moving together, Antoine only a yard or two behind her to her left. It was almost as if he were guiding her in a dance, his own steps unfaltering and absolutely safe.

'That was marvellous — absolutely wonderful!' she cried, as they reached the bottom of the ski-lift and paused, leaning on their batons for a brief rest. 'This is such *fun*, Antoine!'

'And you look so lovely when you are happy!' he replied.

'I've never been so happy!' Jackie said, breathing deeply. 'It is quite impossible to describe how I feel — as if for the first time in my life I am free. It's like flying — as if I were a bird, freed from gravity. Oh, it's the most wonderful feeling in the world!'

'It is like making love!' Antoine said, his voice close against her ear. 'Come with me, Jackie — come to our ski-hut. There we will make this day quite, quite perfect.'

The smile left Jackie's face. This time she was not angry — the happiness, the feeling of gratitude to Antoine for making this day perfect, prevented anger. In any event, his voice was not challenging, teasing, even provocative. It was gentle — kind — full of tenderness for her.

'I *will* come to the hut — for a little

while. But — ' her voice faltered. She knew it must be said. Her own code of behaviour forbade making promises she did not intend to keep. Once Chris had said, 'There's nothing so horrible as a tease,' and she had agreed. 'I won't make love the way you want me to,' she said quietly.

Antoine laughed, suddenly and unexpectedly.

'All right, so we make tea instead. Come, follow me, Jackie!'

Before she could argue, he had turned swiftly on his skis and was already disappearing down the start of the next descent — through the fir trees.

The going was not so easy since the skiers had made a deeply rutted track through the soft snow. Jackie felt a moment's fear as she rounded a bend a little too quickly for safety. Then she saw Antoine ahead of her and drew off the track into the soft snow beside him.

'It is this way to the hut!' he said, pointing his baton to the trees over on their right.

They were walking now, parallel to the mountain side. Their breath came from their mouths like steam from boiling kettles. There was only a glimmer of sun through the immensely tall trees and Jackie felt a new emotion. It was not exactly fear — for one could not be afraid so close to this man who was born and brought up on these mountains. It was more a kind of dwarfing of the spirit, feeling so tiny and helpless in the thick of these huge towering trees. When they stopped for a rest, there was complete and absolute silence. No shouts could be heard from the ski-run — not even the click of the cable car pulley as it ran over the junctions of the wire. There was only the occasional soft thud of snow as it slipped off the branches of pine needles, thawing in places where the hot sun reached it.

'It's another world!' Jackie thought aloud.

Antoine nodded. It was indeed possible to believe that no one else in the world existed. He touched her hand and moved off.

Jackie was beginning to get tired when, rounding a bend, she suddenly saw the little pine-log hut. On her previous visit she had been too cold, too frightened to notice it. Now there was no mist and the slanting rays of the sinking sun touched on the snow covered roof, turning it pink and gold like a Hansel and Gretel story picture.

Antoine unfastened his skis with one quick practised gesture and then bent to unfasten Jackie's. He lifted both pairs of skis and propped them up against the side of the hut, banging them against one another to free them from snow.

'Later there will be a full moon,' he said. 'We will ski down the rest of the way by moonlight. This will be a new experience for you.'

'You mean, it is really bright enough to ski by?' Jackie asked as Antoine pushed open the door.

'But yes! With the moon's reflection

on the snow it is almost like daylight — but much more romantic. It will be something to remember all your life — to tell your children and grandchildren.'

Jackie laughed but Antoine, bending down to light the fire, glanced over his shoulder, his face serious.

'You will not forget, Jackie. Perhaps that is why I wish so much to bring you here. This one day in our lives will belong to us — to no one else. When you are a very old little lady you will remember this and perhaps feel a little sorry that there were not other days just like it.'

Jackie watched his face as he bent over the fire once more, her eyes wide with thoughtfulness. Perhaps Antoine was right — some days were somehow quite special — days one put away in one's memory like a treasure in a box. One single day out of a lifetime. Antoine wanted it perfect and in a way, she, too, wanted it to go on — to complete itself. It was almost as if she were halfway down the mountain knowing that the next half must be done, excited, and yet afraid too.

Presently, the smoking wood burst into flames and Jackie knelt down, drawing off her mittens to warm her fingers. Her hands were clumsy and Antoine seeing her fumbling, at once did the job for her. As her hands were bared, he took them up to his lips and held them there.

Jackie's heart began to beat faster. This was a gentle, humble Antoine she could not dislike and who had the power to awaken all the nerves of her body.

He drew her down beside him and pulled off her woollen ski-cap, fluffing out her hair and holding his warm hand against her cold cheek.

'So beautiful!' he murmured. 'You are so lovely, my Jacqueline!'

His voice gave her name the long French intonation and seemed somehow like a caress.

'He wants me — and I want him!'

Jackie thought with a sudden deep despair. Then, as he began to unbutton her anorak, she felt the fear leave her. In its place came a kind of helplessness. This whole day had been magical, pre-ordained. It had in it the quality of complete impulsiveness. Each thing they had done had been the right thing for this particular day, for each other. There had been no quarrelling, no discord, only harmony. It was not possible to break that harmony, that inevitability, by fighting him now.

She lay still and trembling while he undressed her before the fire. She could hear his quick breathing but he did not speak and somehow she did not wish him to. She closed her eyes and felt his mouth, burning hot, against her body.

'No, no!' she breathed the words, but he did not listen to them, knowing already from the touch of her that she wanted what was to happen; that she had closed her mind to the consequences, the moral issues, the conventions, and allowed her emotions to take control.

He felt a moment's shame. He had planned, worked for this moment but now it was here, the completeness of her surrender confused him. He had expected her to fight him — to have, perhaps, to persuade her against her own will. Now her arms were soft and warm around his bare back; she was all sweetness, all innocence, all his and he could not prevent that moment of shame. In a way, the cards had been stacked against her from the beginning. He knew too much about women — she knew too little about men; too little even about herself.

'You will have to show me!' she whispered.

Then he forgot his scruples for it was also for him a new experience. The women he usually made love to were as wise as he — sometimes wiser. For the first time in his life, he knew the responsibility and delight in taking a young girl, teaching her. And so, grateful to her, he was gentle.

When next he opened his eyes, it was to see tears on Jackie's face. He said quickly:

'Forgive me. I did not want to hurt you.'

But she was silent, having no words to explain to him that it was not for any physical hurt she was crying. The hurt was in her own mind. Already she was regretting desperately what had happened.

Antoine dressed quickly and began to fill a kettle with snow so that he could make coffee. Jackie, longing now for privacy, hurriedly pulled on her clothes and then knelt close to the fire as a shiver ran through her body. She watched Antoine silently, trying to make sense of her haphazard thoughts. She could not dislike him. He had been gentle and unselfish, anxious to please her and give her the same delight he knew himself. No, it was herself she hated for she knew without any shadow of a doubt that she did not love this man. Her body had been hungry for his body but her secret soul had not wanted to betray the man she really loved — Chris.

Antoine made no effort to talk. He was suddenly ill at ease and the excitement of the last half-hour had given way to a completely new feeling of shame. He should have realized that Jackie would not take a few moments of passion casually. For her, in her innocence, what had happened was a momentous step in her life. Dimly, he was aware of it and her silence added to his confusion. He wanted to see her smile reassuringly; to hear her tell him that she was all right and that she thought he was wonderful. Yet he knew instinctively that she was not thinking of him at all. Her expression was withdrawn, far away and a tiny flame of jealousy seared through him as he remembered the adored fiancé, Christopher. Until now, this unknown man had been something near to a joke — someone with whose name he could tease and taunt Jackie, waiting for the angry blush that would always spread into her cheeks as she rose in defence of him and the love they shared.

'Will any girl ever love me as she loves him?'

The thought was vague, unsettling and he thrust it from him.

He wished suddenly that they had not come here to the hut, that they had gone back to the hotel and were even now sitting at the bar, laughing, sharing a drink. Then he shrugged his shoulders, knowing that he would not have been happy even then. He had wanted her — so much that he could not get her out of his mind. It had nothing to do with wanting a woman. From the way Veronica had looked at him once or twice, he'd known he could have had her whenever he wished. But no — it was Jackie he wanted, and now he knew why — because she had been unobtainable. Even now, when the physical act was over, she was no more his than before. Her thoughts, her love, were still with that other man.

He spilt a little of the boiling water as he poured it over the coffee grounds and swore under his breath. Life was not always so simple as he had believed. Now, when he should be feeling triumphant, he could not rid himself of a feeling of shame.

'Jacqueline?'

She looked into his questioning face as she took the hot coffee from him and attempted a smile. There was no anger in her directed at him — only at herself. She had not even the excuse that he had forced her into something she did not wish. When the moment had come, she had given herself freely to him and because of this, she felt her betrayal of Christopher to be even worse.

'Nothing will ever be the same again!'

She did not realize that she had spoken aloud until she heard Antoine say:

'Not quite the same — but perhaps better, *chérie*.'

'Better?'

'Perhaps. Now you understand the

unknown. This should make things easier for you. The biggest bridge is crossed, no? For the next time, you will understand better what it is you need — what a man must have when he loves a girl. A few kisses — this is only the beginning, the tiniest part of his need to possess her.'

She thought suddenly:

'If it had happened with Chris, I should not be sorry!' But the thought could not help.

It was nearly dark now in the hut. Antoine lit a small oil lamp and the room became suddenly warmer, less alien. He sat down again, this time close to her so that he could hold her hand.

'You must not be sorry!' he said urgently. 'No matter what you may be thinking now, we have not committed any crime. I cannot bear to see you looking like this — so unhappy.'

She thought:

'He, too, is sorry!' and was surprised. She would have expected him to be pleased that he had got what he wanted. She could not know that it was her very innocence that shamed him, nor that this feeling would not endure beyond the moment when his desire for her returned. He did not know it himself at this time and he was easily kind.

'Smile for me, Jacqueline! The world has not come to an end, you know. And this was to be our so-happy day, remember?'

She wanted to smile but there was no joy behind it.

'Could we go back — to the hotel!' she asked tentatively.

Antoine shook his head.

'Not yet, I am afraid. It is now quite dark and ski-ing through the trees would be dangerous. In an hour or so, the moon will be full and then we shall go.'

Jackie was suddenly desperately tired. Unaccustomed to the exercise, the day's ski-ing had exhausted her far more than she had realized. Her whole body had begun to ache and she longed for a hot bath. Despite the heat now coming from the log fire, she was shivering.

Antoine took her hands and rubbed them one by one in his own. He was afraid of her silence, her thoughts and longed to talk, to laugh with her — find again that heady excitement of the day. But in the end, it was only his own voice he heard, telling Jackie about his childhood. At first, it had been carefree and full of innocent enjoyment. He went to the village school and, through the season, skied whenever he could. In the hotel, guests made a fuss of him, spoilt him, he admitted, giving him money for ices and chocolates and standing him coco-colas at the hotel bar.

Jackie forgot herself listening to him. She began to see clearly the picture of his childhood. Immensely pretty, the women even then had been unable to resist him. At the age of fifteen, one of the hotel guests had invited him up to her bedroom and introduced him to the delight of sex. Even Antoine, as he talked to Jackie, did not call it love. And so from one hotel guest to another. In the summer when the snow was gone, the hotel filled with a new crowd who came for the golf. Widows, divorcees and even married women welcomed Antoine in their beds. Sex had ceased to mean anything serious to him.

'Until I meet you, Jacqueline. Somehow with you, it was all different.'

He did not tell her why. He was only half aware of the reason, or reasons. Her youth, her unspoilt virginal quality; perhaps, most of all, her resistance. With other women he would not be sharing a bottle of champagne, laughing, carefree, casually intimate.

He was almost frightened when Jackie suddenly put out a hand and touched his arm, saying gently:

'Poor Antoine!'

Her pity, incomprehensible to her, was even less comprehensible to him.

She did not know how to explain but could she have understood her feelings, she would have told him that she was equally sorry for them both. For Antoine because sex had come to have so little real meaning for him; it had lost its freshness and beauty in a series of sordid affairs; he had been corrupted. For herself because she had known it was wrong to give herself to a man she did not love and yet had been too weak to live up to her ideals.

Antoine shrugged his shoulders. He was beginning to feel a little impatient with Jackie. He had been so sure once victory was his, Jackie would be his adoring slave; willing to come when he beckoned. Now it seemed she was somehow turning the tables on him. He was not despising her a little — she was despising him.

But this was nonsense! he told himself, reaching for his mouth organ and beginning to play a Swiss folk song. Jackie was just tired. It was reaction. Tomorrow everything would be different. She needed a good night's sleep, and in the morning she would meet him with a smile and a question in her eyes. She was, after all, a woman like all the rest.

There was still one whole week left before she went home. They would have fun together, enjoy that week and she would go home sad and regretful that she had wasted so much of her holiday.

So he comforted himself, reassured himself, unaware that he craved her good opinion, her admiration, her affection. For the first time in his young life, he had met a girl he respected; in fact, he had met a girl who could move him to love.

5

'Oh, Chris, Chris!' She clung to him, half crying, half laughing. Neither of them noticed the milling crowds in the Airport arrivals lounge.

Chris held Jackie tight for a brief moment, smiling down at her and then linked his arm in hers, saying:

'It's wonderful to have you home, darling!'

Jackie followed him out to the car, her heart brimming with happiness and excitement.

Once they were clear of the airport, Chris said:

'You're looking marvellous, Jackie — so brown and well. It *was* a good idea for you to go away although I've missed you terribly. Tell me all your news, darling. I want to hear all about everything. Your postcards, though numerous, were not very instructive.'

'Not yet — I'll tell you everything later,' Jackie said quickly with a sudden little stab of unease clouding her radiant happiness. 'Tell me first about you — I feel as if I've been away years and years.'

As he talked in his slow quiet way about his job and the visit he had paid each weekend to her mother, Jackie studied him as if she were seeing him for the first time. He looked exactly the same — clean, young, completely familiar and very very dear to her. How could she have forgotten him even for a moment! Already Antoine's face had receded into the past. His expression had been sulky and petulant as he had waved goodbye this morning from the hotel. How bitter his voice had been when he had said, 'So you won, Jacqueline.' As if there had been some kind of battle . . .

'I won't think about him,' Jackie told herself, reaching for Chris's hand where it lay on the wheel of the old Austin. It felt warm and strong beneath her own.

'Don't you agree?' Chris said.

'Agree about what?'

He laughed easily.

'I don't believe you were listening, darling. Were you back in Switzerland?'

'I was thinking how much I love you,' Jackie said, and it was true. So she had been until the memory of Antoine interceded.

Chris's voice deepened.

'I love you, too, darling. I've missed you *desperately*. Oh, Jackie, I've been thinking such a lot about us since you've been away. I no longer think it is such a good idea to wait until we can afford the house before we get married. Frankly, darling, I hated everything while you were gone. Even the job seemed unbearable. The fact is, I want you with me all the time. What I'm really trying to say is, will you marry me right away? I mean as soon as we can arrange it?'

Her eyes grew enormous with surprise and excitement.

'Oh, Chris, yes, *yes!*'

She would have liked him to stop the car so that she could hug him with sheer delight, sheer happiness. It was so exactly what she had wanted him to say; what she herself wanted to do. Rona had been right after all — the brief separation had done Chris good!

'I did have a chat with your mother and she seemed very pleased with the idea of letting us have the big front room until we get our own house. I hope you didn't mind me talking to her about it, darling.'

'Oh, Chris, you silly fool! As if I could mind. You can't begin to know how happy you've made me. I was beginning to think you were having second thoughts about wanting to marry me. Before I went away, I used to wonder how we could be so close in thought about everything else and so far apart over the question of marriage. *I* didn't want to wait — *you* did.'

'Well, I've thought better of it!' Chris said grinning.

'I suppose you'll think me an idiot

but once or twice while you were away, I had nightmare thoughts of losing you. I began to wonder if you might not meet someone else — fall madly in love and come home to tell me you wanted your freedom. I thought how empty and meaningless life would be if that did happen. Perhaps I'm doing the wrong thing but the truth is, I can't risk losing you again, Jackie. It's been a sort of hell in some ways. I kept thinking how attractive you are . . . how mad I was ever to let you go.'

'You *made* me go!' Jackie said softly.

'Yes, I suppose I did. But seeing you now looking so fit and well, I think I was right to do so. All the same, never again — not without me.'

It was a new Chris — this ardent, possessive lover she had wanted him to be. She was more deeply in love with him than ever and wildly excited about the thought of being married to him so soon.

Her mother had prepared a welcome home supper for the three of them round the sitting room fire. There was even a bottle of white wine to go with the chicken.

Chris was in wonderful form. Every now and again he would give her a long searching look as if she were a little strange to him and his voice and eyes held the same note of excitement.

'I hardly recognize you, darling. You look different somehow. Maybe it's the tan — or that new way you are doing your hair.'

When her mother had gone tactfully to bed, Chris took her in his arms and kissed her. It was a long lover's kiss, searching, demanding. At once Antoine's face rose into Jackie's mind. She felt the same quick breathless stirring of her senses and for a moment fought against her mounting desire until she remembered that this was Chris — she didn't need to fight *him*. There was no need to feel guilty in wanting Chris . . .

She knew that he did want her. This time he did not draw away from her, reminding her that they must 'be careful' as he had so often done in the past. It was Jackie who broke away, feeling that in some strange way she was not entitled to this new wave of love and desire from Chris — not until she had confessed to him that she had let Antoine make love to her; not until Chris had forgiven her.

She drew him down beside her on the sofa and sat a little apart from him. Then she said quietly:

'There's something I want to tell you, Chris — something about me . . .'

He looked down at her flushed, serious face and smiled very tenderly.

'Dearest, you don't have to explain yourself to me. Don't you think I know what it is you want to tell me!'

'You — you know?'

Her eyes were enormous with surprise.

His voice was very gentle, very loving.

'I think so. You're worried because sometimes your emotions get out of control. That's quite normal, darling.

When two people love each other the way we do, sex does rear its ugly head in no uncertain terms. There's nothing wrong in our wanting each other so much. When we get married, we won't be under this kind of strain.'

He took her hand and played with her fingers. He hoped he had reassured her but she stayed silent. He said:

'Surely you don't think it's any different for me? Sometimes it has been terribly hard for me to keep calm. But in one way, I suppose it was easier because I've always felt responsible for you . . . wanted to protect you from myself. That has helped me to prevent us going too far. You see, I do love you so much, Jackie. I want our marriage to be perfect. Somehow it would spoil things if before we were married we gave way to a moment's hungry passion. I've always thought that for a girl especially, the wedding night ought to be beautiful and romantic and the start of a completely new life for her — the real moment of becoming a woman of giving herself up to a man to love and to cherish.'

'Oh, Chris!'

She felt anxious and ashamed and suddenly utterly unworthy of him. The fact that she had given way to Antoine appalled her even more knowing now that Chris had restrained his ardour to protect her. And she had thought him cold and unresponsive!

'Oh, Chris . . . ' she murmured remorsefully. 'I'm not sure we should get married now. You've put me on a pedestal where I've no right to be. If you knew I had stepped down from it, you might stop loving me.'

He put his arms round her and held her firmly by the shoulders.

'Silly! As if you *could* fall short of my ideal. You're all I've ever wanted, Jackie — *all I shall ever want.*'

She would have given her right hand to be able to say the same to him knowing it was the truth. But she had wanted Antoine — and Chris had been forgotten when her conscience had been stilled in that tormenting moment of desire.

'Jackie, you haven't stopped loving me?'

His voice was suddenly anxious.

'No, no, *no*! I think I love you more than ever, Chris. I shall always love you. It's just that . . . Chris, I do want to explain something to you — something about myself. Out there in Switzerland it was all so beautiful — the sun and snow and everyone gay and happy. But at times I was terribly lonely. I was asked to go out dancing by the son of the owner of the hotel and . . . '

She stopped as Chris put a hand over her lips.

'Darling, don't say any more. I don't mind if you went out with other men. I never expected you to sit alone in the hotel knitting. I realized Mrs. Cairgorn would probably include you in her parties and I was glad you could have some fun. Did you really believe I would resent the fact that you enjoyed yourself?'

She swallowed and tried once more

to confess. But every word Chris spoke only made her feeling of treachery worse. Her confession died on her lips as Chris said:

'Why should I have worried, darling? I trusted you just as you knew you could trust me. When two people love as we do, there's no room for petty jealousies. We have faith in each other.'

Tears were stinging her eyelids. She bit hard on her lip to stop them falling and decided that she would tell Chris another time — tomorrow perhaps. Nothing must spoil tonight. She couldn't bear to hurt him, disillusion him.

'So long as you love me, Jackie, nothing in the whole wide world matters — *nothing!*' he said finally, and took her back into his arms.

He left an hour later, smiling and glowing with happiness. But there was no smile on Jackie's face as she went up to bed.

Could she ever tell Chris? How could she expect him to understand when she couldn't understand herself. Now, far away from Antoine's compelling personality, from the temptation of his constant proximity and determined demands, her emotions were inexplicable. Perhaps, she thought with despair as she brushed her hair and prepared for bed, she was not really in love with Chris. But that was absurd! She was more in love with him than she had ever been. She wanted to be his wife — wanted it with a great burning need and Chris now wanted her in the same way. There was to be no more waiting, no more having to keep her emotions subdued. From next month on, she would be able to share her days and nights with Chris and they would never have to be parted again.

She climbed into bed and turned out the light. But she could not sleep yet. A new thought had crept into her mind. Perhaps, after all, there was no need to tell Chris anything. Her brief affair with Antoine was all over now. She would never see him again. If Chris knew and was jealous, he might not be able to forget 'the other man' in her life as easily as she could. Antoine might become an unfortunate ghost haunting their happiness. It would certainly destroy the complete faith and belief in her which Chris held and she couldn't bear it if he stopped loving her.

'I'm being cowardly again!' she told herself angrily. It was far better that Chris should know the real her — the girl who was too weak to resist a pure infatuation of the senses; a girl whose love for her fiancé counted for so little that the moment he was out of sight she could be fatally attracted to another man. Was this the kind of wife Chris wanted or deserved?

She fell asleep at last, her mind still uncertain and full of a strange anguish which spread into her dreams so that she woke tired and unrefreshed to the new day.

* * *

'I'm glad you're going to keep on working for a bit,' Rona said as they sat in the rest room drinking coffee and waiting for the first of the afternoon's clients. She looked at her friend and gave her a friendly nudge with her arm. 'You must be frantically excited. I'm dying to hear what made your Chris change his mind.'

Jackie smiled. It was her first day back at work and the morning had been so busy she hadn't had a chance to gossip with Rona.

'I think you were right — he missed me!' she said. 'It's to be next month, Rona, and, of course, I want you for my number one bridesmaid. If you can spare the time I thought you might like to come with me on Wednesday afternoon and choose my frock and the bridesmaids' dresses. There won't be time to have them made.'

Rona leant back in her chair and sighed happily.

'Of course I'll come, ducks! Nothing I'd enjoy more. You'll wear white, won't you!' She giggled. 'After all, you at least can do so with a clear conscience so you might as well. Jackie, shall you ask the Cairgorn woman to the wedding? I mean, will you have to?'

'I don't know. I hadn't thought about it. I suppose I might. She's coming in to have her hair re-tinted at four so maybe I will ask her, but I don't suppose my wedding will interest her much.'

'But you'll be such a beautiful bride!' Rona said irrelevantly.

She chatted on asking Jackie questions about her holiday and finally said:

'But what did you do all the time — while *she* was gadding around, I mean? Surely you didn't just sit!'

To her surprise, Jackie blushed. Then Rona laughed.

'I do believe you've been a naughty girl. You met someone, didn't you, Jackie? Come on, out with it. Who was he? What happened? Tell Aunty all.'

Jackie turned away and busied herself with the perming tray which had already been tidied by young Sue.

'Don't make it sound so mysterious, Rona. I did go out dancing and ski-ing once or twice with a young man called Antoine de Verre. He was the son of the man who owned the hotel and a wonderful skier. That's all there was to it.'

'Then why the blush?' asked Rona astutely. 'Come clean, Jackie. You can trust me. Did you fall just the smallest little bit in love? Was he handsome? Is Chris madly jealous? I'll bet that's what made him speed up the wedding plans.'

'No, it isn't!' Jackie said sharply. 'I — I haven't even told him about Antoine.'

'Then there was something more in it than you've made out. Well, I won't press you if you don't want to confide.'

Jackie hesitated. She didn't want to think about Antoine, far less talk about him. And yet Rona was so sensible and by comparison with herself, experienced. Maybe she would advise Jackie if she *ought* to tell Chris.

'No, I *want* to tell you,' she said. 'But there won't be time now. We'll have a cup of tea over the road when the shop shuts. I'll tell you then.'

'Jacqueline!' It was Mr. Paul's voice. 'Your lady is here.'

Jackie hurried to her feet and out into the salon which was already filling up with customers.

The first hour passed quickly and then Veronica Cairgorn came into the salon. She was dressed entirely in black and looked extremely smart. She greeted Jackie with a piercing cry of welcome which made Rona and the other girls smile and poor Jackie blush with embarrassment.

'I've masses to tell you!' she said in her loud voice. 'It can wait till I've been washed. Mind my make-up, Sue — I've just been done. Stupid, really, to have a face-do before a tinting, but I couldn't get an appointment earlier. Why don't you have a course on beauty treatment, Jackie, so you can 'do' me?'

She had to stop talking while Sue washed her hair and then Jackie took over again.

'My dear, you'll never guess what

happened after you left Crans. Your poor young man attached himself to *me*. Not that there is anything very pathetic about Antoine, mark you! All the same, I think your rejection of him was a very nasty blow to his pride, Jackie. I only hope your young man appreciates it!'

'Chris and I are going to be married next month!' Jackie blurted out, half defiantly, half proudly.

Veronica raised her eyebrows.

'Congratulations,' she drawled. 'Then it won't disappoint you if I tell you that your Swiss boy friend is fast recovering from the broken heart you left behind you. He joined our party after you left and insisted upon twisting with me — magnificently, I might add — until the early hours. Frankly, Jackie, I think you were a bit of a fool. I found him devastating, even if he was a bit of a bore the way he kept harping on you. If you'd played your cards right, I think he might even have married you.'

'But I didn't want to marry him,'

Jackie protested.

'Ah, no, I keep forgetting you're already engaged. Your fiancé must be quite something if he puts our Antoine in the shade. Oh, well, it's your life. Which reminds me, as the saying goes, in the midst of life we are in death — you may not have noticed it, Jackie, but I'm wearing black. I'm a widow — a damn wealthy one too. My old man made a sudden and not unexpected departure yesterday. That's why I had to get my hair done this afternoon. The funeral's tomorrow.'

Jackie was deeply shocked. Of course, she had known Mr. Cairgorn was very ill but Veronica's casual announcement and apparent indifference to his death appalled her. Even if Veronica did not love him, she could at least have shown some outward sign of being sorry that he had died. Perhaps a show of grief would be hypocritical! All the same, it was shocking to hear her announce such news in her gay, everyday voice.

Seeing the younger girl's expression, Veronica said:

'There's no point in pretending in this life, Jackie. I was never in love with Carlton and he knew it. His death doesn't affect me in the least except to set me free from a bond that was becoming extremely tiresome.'

Jackie could think of nothing to say. She put the last curler in Veronica's hair and tied on the net in silence.

Veronica said:

'I hope to get abroad again next week. Antoine told me the hotel closes next month and it is usually very gay there just before they shut up shop. I'm sorry you won't be coming with me. Useless to invite you, no doubt, if you're about to get married?'

'No, no, I couldn't possibly come!' Jackie said quickly. Not even the thought of the sun and the snow and all the luxuries could tempt her even for a second. It was such a relief to be safe at home; at peace with herself and Chris . . . or almost at peace. She had still not found a chance to tell Chris about Antoine de Verre. Maybe she could bring up his name when she told him tonight about Veronica.

She handed Veronica over to Sue to put under the drier and went thoughtfully back to the rest room. Strange that Veronica should be going back to Crans. Perhaps the friends she had made in the hotel would still be there and had wanted her to rejoin them. If it had not been for Mr. Cairgorn's sudden death, she might not have come home at all.

Jackie shivered again, suddenly depressed and unsure of herself and life. How was it possible for a woman like Veronica to be so indifferent to the death of her own husband! She must have had some affection for him when she married him. Jackie knew from personal experience that Veronica could be very generous and affectionate at times — she wasn't all bad. Jackie didn't wish to be narrow minded and it had seemed to her in Switzerland that to condemn Veronica for her moral outlook was wrong. Just because Veronica had a different set of values didn't mean she was wicked. She excused Veronica's behaviour to herself on the grounds that this was pretty universal amongst the rich society set in which Veronica moved. She and her friends thought nothing of having love affairs — even if they or the men they chose were married. Veronica had laughed and teased her about her determination to keep herself for one man only — for Chris.

Maybe Veronica was more honest; she refused to be hypocritical about the death of a man she didn't love. And she gave way to men she found attractive because she saw no harm in it. Jackie was less honest, really. She still had not been able to bring herself to tell Chris . . .

She felt suddenly tired and unhappy. Her meeting with Veronica had once more confused her thinking. The fact that she loved Chris and wanted to marry him was the only thing she was really certain about. She wished she could stop thinking about Veronica and Crans and Antoine.

Rona came in and gave her a passing glance.

'What's up, Jackie? Seen a ghost?'

Jackie gave an uncertain smile.

'Maybe!' she said, thinking once more of Antoine. But because she was not as honest as Veronica, she added:

'Mrs. Cairgorn's husband has just died. Hearing it like that was a bit of a shock!'

Rona, and later Chris, accepted this reason for her pale face and subdued manner.

'What a cheat I am!' Jackie thought, as Chris took her in his arms and stroked her hair tenderly with his strong warm hands.

'I'll be glad when you stop working at that shop,' Chris said irrelevantly. 'I think it's too much for you being on your feet all day coping with spoilt women like Veronica Cairgorn. Maybe next year . . .'

'But I don't mind working — I enjoy it,' Jackie said truthfully. 'Besides, we will need the money for a bit, Chris, you know that. Don't worry about me . . . I'm perfectly all right.'

She was frightened that he had sensed her confusion and inward unrest. Now . . . *now* was the time to tell him.

'Chris . . . ' she began, 'Veronica is going back to Crans. She made a lot of friends in the hotel, you know, including the young man I went out with. Remember I told you about him?'

Chris moved his hand to her shoulder and dropped a quick kiss on the side of her neck.

'Did you, sweetheart? How beautiful you smell, Jackie. Is it a new perfume? I do love you so much.'

'But, Chris . . . '

'Kiss me!'

She shivered and then turned her face upwards for his kiss. Her mother had gone up to bed and they were alone on the customary sofa in front of the fire. It was warm and cosy and the firelight played on their faces. Chris looked almost tanned in the glow and his face was taut and a little fierce with longing. Jackie had a sudden frightened impression that it wasn't Chris at all, kissing her, whispering those words of love, straining her to him. It was Antoine.

She pulled herself away with a smothered cry and covered her face with her hands.

'Jackie, *darling* . . . what's wrong? Did I frighten you? Jackie — what's happened?'

She flung herself back into his arms, kissing him frantically — like a small child. She was nearly crying and he frowned, failing to understand what was wrong so suddenly between them.

Then she said:

'Nothing's wrong — nothing! I just wish we were married now — this minute. I don't think I can stand much more of this — this waiting!'

He relaxed at once and hugged her

with relief. This was something he could understand. Before Jackie had gone away, he had firmly anchored his emotions into a kind of rut where he could manage them, keep them under control. But he had missed her so terribly and seeing her again, more beautiful to him than ever, more mysterious and unknown, had altered everything. He knew that his plan to wait until they could afford a house was no longer of prime importance. He wanted her — wanted to make love to her — to have her with him all the time, to know that she was his, his love and his wife. This month before the actual wedding was going to be almost harder to bear than the three preceding years. No wonder Jackie's nerves were on edge . . . His own were, too, and he wasn't sleeping well or eating much.

'It won't be long now, darling!' he whispered. 'Our banns are being called for the first time this Sunday. We're going to be so happy together. I don't think you begin to know how much I love you. I'll take such care of you, darling. You'll be the most spoilt and beloved wife.'

'Chris, don't! I don't deserve it. I'm not really any different from any other girl. Don't put me on that pedestal of yours. I couldn't bear it when you found I was just ordinary after all.'

'As if you could be!' Chris said almost angrily. 'You *are* different, Jackie. Don't imagine I go around with my eyes shut. The typists in the bank for instance — some of them even younger than you are — they'll sleep with practically any man who wants them. While you were away, one of them . . . oh, I'd rather not talk about it. I just know that you would never behave like that — you have too much pride and decency in you. Perhaps I'm old-fashioned but I'd hate to think the girl I married had played around with other men. Or maybe I'm just selfish — I don't know. I want to be the one to teach you what real love means. You're so innocent, Jackie — you probably don't know what I am talking about. Sex is — well, it can be two things — just an appetite one satisfies, or the most beautiful way in the world of expressing love.'

He paused and took one of her cold hands in his two warm ones.

'We've never gone very far, have we, Jackie? A few kisses and caresses. You've known instinctively that something was missing and I often sensed your longing to go much further than we did. I never let it because it can so easily get out of control. You're not a cold person and the way I feel about you, we might not have been able to call a halt. But you will be glad, darling, when the time comes for us really to belong I shall be so gentle with you — you never need be frightened with me. You'll be able to share something with me you've never shared with anyone else.'

He could not know how he was tormenting her. He idealised her and while this was flattering in one way, no one knew better than Jackie that she was a perfectly ordinary girl with ordinary feelings and no special virtues. Now he made her feel frighteningly guilty and inadequate.

'Chris, I don't think I can marry you. You don't understand. I can't marry you — I can't!'

6

'Happy the bride the sun shines on!' said Uncle Julian jovially. He was standing in the sitting room staring out of the window at the pale gold of the April sunshine filtering across the street.

A few moments ago, Mrs. Kemster had left for the church. She had given one last look at Jackie's veil and gown and beamed happily.

'You look so beautiful, my darling. No bride ever looked lovelier.'

Uncle Julian was to give her away. Although he was her father's brother, he lived far away in Newcastle and was almost a stranger to his niece.

'If my own father had been here now, perhaps I could have told him — asked him to help me!' Jackie thought frantically. But her father was dead and she couldn't tell a stranger she didn't want to get married after all; that she was frightened and unhappy and wanted only to run miles and miles away.

Her long white wedding gown flowed round her, hiding the trembling of her legs. The white misty veil made her feel even more as if she were lost in some terrible unreal fog. The bouquet of white and yellow rose buds was shaking in her cold grasp.

'You look a bit pale. Not feeling faint, my dear?' Uncle Julian asked anxiously.

She shook her head.

'Car should be here soon. Don't want to get to church too early . . . keep 'em waiting a bit, eh?'

His voice droned on and Jackie's mind slipped back over the past few weeks.

'Don't be such a silly little fool, Jackie!' Rona's voice, matter of fact, sensible, sure of herself. 'Anyone would think you'd led a wildly promiscuous life the way you go on. You love him and that's all your precious Chris will worry about.'

'It isn't just that, Rona. Chris thinks I'm perfect. If he knew I'd let Antoine make love to me, he wouldn't want to marry me. I'm not good enough for him. He might find out what I'm really like and . . . '

'And what are you like? A warm-blooded passionate female who wanted a man. What's wrong in that? You're just normal, Jackie. I don't know why you don't tell him about Antoine and have done with it, though personally, I think those sort of confessions are a bit silly. But since you're letting it prey on your mind, at least give *Chris* the chance to decide whether he still wants to marry you or not.'

'I've tried to tell him. He just doesn't listen. Every time I begin he breaks in to say how good or innocent or pure I am. He won't let me tell him, Rona . . . '

She could hear in her mind Chris's voice, angry and distressed.

'You say you aren't in love with anyone else, so *why* can't you marry me? You love me . . . you said you loved me. Have you stopped all of a sudden? Why can't we be married?'

'You don't understand, Chris. I do

153

love you but I don't think you really love me . . . not the *real* me. I think if you knew what I'm like inside you wouldn't want to marry me.'

Chris had laughed, greatly relieved.

'That, surely, is for me to decide. As to my not knowing you — that's ridiculous. I've known you for three years. You might as well say I don't know myself. You're sure this isn't just an excuse — Jackie. Sure you haven't stopped loving me?'

'It'll all be all right once the wedding is over, Jackie!' Her mother's voice, calm and certain. 'Every girl gets last minute nerves. You'll see, darling. So stop being such a silly girl. Chris loves you and you love him. That's all that matters.'

All that matters . . . all that matters . . . trust me . . . silly girl . . . I love you, Chris . . . tonight . . .

'Ah, there's the car. Ready, my dear?'

Not much traffic — Saturday afternoon — people are staring — I suppose it's the white ribbon on the car. I remember being confirmed in this church. There's Rona. How nice she looks. 'Thank you, Uncle Julian. Hullo, Rona.' The sun is still shining. Now I must go in — walk slowly, slowly . . . I won't look at Chris . . . Rona, take me out . . . no, it's too late now. Mother — how proud you are of your new hat! It looks nice from the back, too. The music has stopped . . . Chris . . . I must listen to what the Vicar is saying.

' . . . *we are gathered together here in the sight of God and in the face of this congregation to join together this Man and this Woman in Holy Matrimony; which is . . .* '

That's me — Chris and me . . . It's so cold . . . I *must* listen . . .

' . . . *therefore is not by any to be enterprised nor taken in hand, unadvisedly, lightly, wantonly, to satisfy . . .* '

Wanton . . . that is the word . . . I behaved wantonly . . . Suppose Antoine were here in the church! Suppose when it comes to the bit about if any man may shew any just cause why they may not lawfully be joined together . . . suppose Antoine were to stand up and say . . .

' . . . *ordained for the procreation of children, to be brought up in the fear and nurture of the Lord* . . . '

I wish it was over! What is Chris thinking? Can God bless a marriage which begins like this? I ought to have told Chris . . . made him understand. Help me, God! I want to make Chris happy. I want to be a good wife.

' . . . *Wilt thou have this Woman to thy wedded wife* . . . '

How strong Chris's voice sounds. His hand feels warm — warm. I am so cold.

' . . . *Wilt thou obey him, and serve him, love honour and keep him in sickness and in health; and forsaking all other, keep thee only unto him, so long as ye both shall live?'*

'I will!'
I will, I will. I swear I will be a good wife, Chris.

Now it is all over. I am Chris's wife, Mrs. Christopher Dershaw. Mother is crying, but she looks happy. So many people. Who are they all? The aisle seems very long. I'm glad I can hold on to Chris's arm. The sun is still shining.

'Would you smile a little, please?'

The flashlight — more photographs. There's our car. No confetti . . . A pity, really . . . Now we're alone.

'Chris?'

'My wife!'

I can't feel anything — his kiss is unreal . . . maybe I'm dreaming this.

'You're all right, my darling? You look so pale.'

Brandy! Wonder where Mother keeps it? Medicine cupboard . . . for emergencies.

'Thanks, Chris!' It tastes horrible . . . we'll never get thirty people into this little house. Poor Mother — there'll be so much clearing up after we've gone. Or perhaps the catering firm will clean up.

'Better stand beside me, dearest — the first guests are arriving.'

'Rona, I feel terrible. I can't go . . . I can't.'

'Now, Jackie, pull yourself together. Look at that scrumptious going away suit of yours — that's a gorgeous blue. Bet you look dreamy in it. Come on, Jackie, let me help.'

'Rona, I'm frightened!'

'Nonsense, silly! You're going to have a wonderful honeymoon. When you come back and I tell you how you're behaving now, you won't believe me. A lamb to the slaughter. You don't know! Put a bit of rouge on — you look like death warmed up.'

'Goodbye — goodbye, Mother, thank you. I'll write. Uncle Julian . . . Rona . . . goodbye . . . '

'Come on, darling, in you get!'

The sunshine had gone. The station was surprisingly empty of people and was large and cold.

'It'll be warm in the carriage!' Chris said. 'I'll try and get an empty one.'

'No, Chris, don't bother, really . . . '

'Bother? I want my wife to myself! Ah, there's the train.'

Chris has been holding my hand ever since we got in the train; he has kissed me three times but I still don't feel anything. Rona said it would be all right. Chris looks so happy. I'll make him happy — it will be all right. Egham next stop. It didn't take long. A good idea not to go too far away — spend the money saved on fares on a really first-class hotel. I wonder what Great Fosters will be like. Sounds so big. Chris said I'd have a surprise? He's so good to me . . . Chris, I love you . . . I love you. My mind loves you . . . only my body is numb . . .

'There, darling. Like it?'

Jackie stood in the doorway and

gazed at the huge room with awe. There was a vast four-poster bed — nearly as big as the room itself, with its dark panelling and leaded light windows. It was lovely . . . but so big, so luxurious. The vase of red roses on the dressing table were dwarfed by the size and the splendour of the room.

She walked over to the flowers and picked up the white card.

'*For my wife with all my love, Chris!*'

He came up behind her and put his arms round her gently.

'I love you, Jackie!'

She turned in the circle of his arms and looked up at him, seeing him properly for the first time that day. This was Chris — the same Chris, except that now he was also her husband.

'Chris?'

His arms tightened round her and she closed her eyes as he began to kiss her. She waited for the familiar pleasure that his kisses, his touch always gave her, but now suddenly she seemed to be outside her own body — like a kind of wraith looking down on their embracing bodies. She saw rather than felt Chris's hands move from her waist to her breasts and rest there, lovingly, tenderly. She stayed still, holding her breath, waiting once more for the breathless sinking sensation that Antoine's touch gave her when he had fondled her the same way. Then Chris's hands slid down past her waist and rested on her hips. The colour had come into his face and he swallowed once or twice as the tension of desire mounted in him.

He wants me — now — not tonight, but now! Jackie thought with sudden frantic fear. She must not fail him — she must want him, too. He would sense her coldness. Why didn't she feel anything, anything at all?

Suddenly his hands fell away from her and he said huskily:

'How selfish I'm being. You must be tired, darling, after all the excitement. Would you like to lie down and rest for a bit? We don't have to go down to dinner yet. Or are you hungry? You didn't eat a thing at the reception — I watched you. I think it all went off quite well, don't you?'

He walked away from her, lifting his suitcase on to the bed and began to unpack. She stood uncertainly watching him.

'It's almost as if he had suddenly become a stranger,' she thought uneasily. 'I feel I ought not to be here — in the same room. Chris is a stranger!'

'What time is it, Chris?'

'Six-thirty. Lie down, darling. I'll unpack for you if you like. There's no need to eat before half-past eight. There's a dance tonight — one every Saturday.'

She turned away from him and began to take off her blue going-away suit. She was too self-conscious to see if Chris was looking at her. Leaving on the nylon petticoat, she slipped under the eiderdown in the huge four-poster bed and tried to concentrate on Chris's voice. But her mind would wander off on its own.

'We're here, alone, and we are married. I ought to be in his arms, as eager as he is to complete our marriage. Suppose I still don't want it tonight? *I mustn't disappoint him*. This is madness, sheer stupidity. Do all girls feel like this or is it just because I have this terrible feeling that I've cheated? Chris doesn't know what I'm really like . . . But if I am 'wanton,' why don't I feel something more now? I love Chris — love him with my whole heart and body and mind. Before I went to Switzerland, I used to long for the time when we could make love properly. Sometimes I couldn't sleep at night for wanting Chris so much. Maybe it's just nerves. Rona, tell me . . . '

She had drifted into a semi-state of sleep. Chris woke her an hour later. He was sitting on the huge bed beside her, looking down at her tenderly.

'Feeling better, darling? You've got some colour back in your cheeks at last.'

He bent and kissed her gently on the

lips. She lifted her arms and wound them round his neck. She *was* feeling better, less tense and nervous. She looked into Chris's eyes and saw the love and tenderness shining there.

'Chris?' It was half a question, half a plea. Now, if he wanted to make love to her, she would not refuse.

He understood at once and the smile left his face as he half lifted her from beneath the eiderdown and began to caress her warm bare shoulders. Watching him, Jackie saw his expression slowly change. Now it was no longer gentle or tender but filled with a fierce gripping desire. She was suddenly once more afraid. She had seen that same look in Antoine's eyes and been afraid of the power he had over her.

'*This is Chris!*' she told herself wildly. 'I am his wife — I need not fight *him* . . .'

She closed her eyes as Chris began to pull the nylon slip over her head. Then she felt his hands on her breasts as he quickly, urgently, removed the last of her clothing. At once, she was back in the ski-hut on the mountain. She could almost smell the wood smoke of the pine logs. The mouth that came down on hers was not Chris's mouth, the touch was now a slowly mounting thrill of excitement and longing. Her body was on fire and she surrendered herself with a complete and stirring abandon. This time, she knew, there would be no last minute refusal. There was no longer any reason to say no.

Across the candlelit table, Chris's face looked radiant with happiness. All through dinner he had stopped to pay her some extravagant compliment; to reach out for her hand; to tell her again and again how happy he was.

Jackie tried desperately to match his mood. She knew that upstairs in that vast rather frightening four-poster bed, she had succeeded in making Chris happy. She knew that he never once doubted that her passionate longing was for him and him alone. What he did not know — and *never* must, was that behind her closed eyes, another man had held her and loved her; taken her and brought her to a new understanding of life. She had betrayed Chris. She felt degraded — and worse still, felt that she had degraded Chris's love which was so pure and true; so unselfish and good.

She felt wretchedly unhappy. She could not share his joy and pleasure and outside it, she felt lonely and afraid.

If Chris sensed her reluctance to return to the privacy of their bedroom, he did not show it. He danced every dance until 'Goodnight, Ladies' and only then suggested that it had been a long, long day and that they should go to bed.

As she lay in the bath, soaking in the hot water in which she had put handfuls of the new bath salts her mother had given her for her honeymoon, Jackie felt near to tears. This was her wedding day and Chris had done everything possible to make it perfect. The hotel was romantic and beautiful, their room like a room in a storybook castle. The dinner had been wonderful and the dancing excitingly different from the tennis club dances and Saturday 'hops' they usually attended. Nothing was wrong and yet everything was wrong because of the barrier in her mind. Perhaps tonight, when she went back to their room, she should tell Chris — try to make him understand. Once he had forgiven her, if he could bring himself to go on loving her, she could feel free to love him as she wanted to. They could stop being two people and become one.

But Chris gave her no chance. He took her at once into his arms and lifting her off her feet, carried her over to the bed. Although he was always gentle and tender, he was impatient too. Slowly her body began to catch fire from his caresses.

'I won't think of anyone else — anything else — except Chris — us . . . ' she thought. But even as she stared into Chris's eager tensed face, the image changed and she knew that Antoine's ghost had come to haunt her once again.

7

The first week in May was gloriously warm. The two girls bought sandwiches and took them into the Park in their lunch hour. Jackie said suddenly:

'It's almost as warm as it was in Switzerland!'

Rona gave her friend a quick look and said:

'You know, Jackie, I've never quite understood what happened to you in Switzerland. That holiday changed you. You've not been the same girl since.'

Jackie turned her face away from Rona's penetrating gaze.

'Not the same?' she asked weakly.

'No! You used to be so gay — always smiling and carefree and happy. Oh, I know you had the occasional tiff with old Chris but it never lasted long and next day you would be the contented, good-tempered Jackie we all know. Do you realize, darling, that you twice bit poor old Sue's head off this morning? It isn't *like* you. Nothing wrong between you and Chris, is there?'

'Of course not!' Jackie said at once. 'How could there be? We've only been back from our honeymoon for a week.'

'I know!' Rona said caustically. 'That's just it. You are hardly the radiant happy bride. Come on, Jackie, tell Auntie Rona. You know there's nothing you can't talk about to me.'

Jackie hesitated. She, herself, knew that things were not as they should be between a newly married couple. Chris was wonderful, of course, but there was a kind of constraint which she could not describe but which she felt. Sometimes she would catch Chris staring at her in a puzzled, uneasy way — as if he was unsure about her. At such moments, she would hurry to him and kiss him quickly as if to reassure him. She couldn't bear him to look unhappy and at once the expression on his face would change and he would say: 'You do really love me, don't you?'

'I love him too much,' Jackie thought now. 'I want him to have everything in life just the way he wants it, and most of all, I want to be the perfect wife.'

Yet that barrier was still there — a little stronger than it had been on their wedding night since each time they made love, she counted it as yet another time she was cheating him. She had still not been able to bring herself to talk about her affair with Antoine. It might have been possible on their wedding night if she had had more courage, but now it had all become too vital to talk about casually. There was no possible way of explaining to Chris in one breath that she loved him desperately and in another that every time they lay in the dark, it was another man's face she saw in her imagination. She couldn't understand it herself, so how could she expect Chris, who idolised her, to understand?

'Well, Jackie? Don't you want to confide? You know I'd never breathe a word to a soul. And if it's about sex, you don't have to be shy with me. Nothing shocks me!'

Jackie gave a half smile.

'You sound like the most experienced woman in the world!' she said. Then her face became taut again. She said suddenly:

'Maybe you were right after all, Rona, and I should have let Chris make love to me before we were married.'

'Then it isn't a success?'

Jackie threw the empty paper bag into the refuse basket behind the bench and lay back against the hard wood, closing her eyes and lifting her face to the sun.

'It isn't Chris!' she said in a whisper. 'It's me. Chris is wonderful — a perfect lover. It's just that . . . oh, I can't explain to you, Rona. You'd only think I'm mad.'

Rona patted Jackie's knee sympathetically.

'Don't talk about it if it upsets you. I don't want to pry. But if that part of the marriage isn't right, then nothing else will be, Jackie. Give yourselves a little more time and if it still doesn't work out, see a doctor, will you?'

'But I couldn't . . . a doctor wouldn't understand. It isn't a physical difficulty — it's mental.'

'Okay!' Rona said cheerfully. 'So what? Doctors can sort out the mind, too. Promise me not to let it go on too long? I think a marriage has to get off on the right foot — otherwise it can create all sorts of problems later which aren't so easy to overcome. Will you, Jackie?'

Jackie nodded. Once or twice she had thought of seeing the family doctor but she had at once told herself he couldn't help. How could a doctor dispel an hallucination? The whole thing seemed mad in broad daylight — too crazy and silly to tell Rona, let alone a medical man. Yet when darkness fell and she was alone with Chris, she knew that the moment he began to touch her and her nervous system awoke to a quick eager response, her eyes would see not Chris's dear beloved face but Antoine's — cruel, determined, ugly with desire.

Because of this, she could not give love. Her nights with Chris were full of wild, furious passion, quickly satisfied, leaving them both with a strange feeling of incompleteness. Although they still clung to one another they were miles apart in mind. Jackie, stiff with remorse and the feeling of having cheated Chris again, would be unable to speak the tender, loving words she longed to say to him. All she really could have cried were: 'Forgive me, forgive me!' and these she could not say knowing the hurt they would inflict.

Chris, in his turn was at a loss. He could not pinpoint what was wrong between them. In the daytime, Jackie was gentle, loving, immensely thoughtful of his wishes and in every way the kind of wife he had expected her to be. But at night, alone with him in bed, she seemed to become a different personality. At first he had rejoiced in her heady, warm response. He had always known that underneath the quiet exterior, she was a passionate woman who only needed awakening. But their love-making lacked some vital element. It was almost a harsh, fierce giving and taking — without gentleness, tenderness — the real quality of love. The two Jackies seemed to him to be quite separate and oddly at variance. He knew he satisfied her physically, as she did him, and yet he was left always with the feeling that they were not close after their love-making but further apart than ever. He tried not to think about it — to accept things as they were, but now and again he would watch her face as she set the table for dinner or sat over her sewing and wonder what she really thought and felt. The remoteness of her expression would make him feel more and more uneasy and then she would look up and jump to her feet unexpectedly and come across the room to kiss him with a strange compelling urgency.

'I love you, I love you!' she would whisper. Once or twice he had wondered who she was trying to convince — him or herself? Then he felt mean for doubting her love. So he would forget his anxiety — until the next time.

Rona glanced now at her watch and sighed.

'Time to get back to the salon, Jackie. I've got a full afternoon. By the way, what's happened to your Mrs. Cairgorn? Still in Switzerland?'

Jackie stood up and nodded.

'I had a card last week. She didn't say much except that the snow was beginning to get very soft.'

It was nearly closing time when Rona came across to Jackie as she set a client's hair and whispered:

'Talk of the devil, Jackie. That was your Mrs. Cairgorn on the phone to Mr. Paul just now. She's home and wants you to go round tomorrow afternoon to set her hair at her house. Must be something special on as Mr. Paul agreed although you were fully booked. I've got two of your regulars. Wonder what's up!'

Jackie wondered, too. She wished she did not have to go. Although Veronica had been very kind to her, Jackie could never feel really friendly towards the older woman. She would have preferred to forget her, along with any reminder of her trip to Switzerland — and Antoine . . .

But when she was shown into Veronica's house next afternoon by the German maid, Veronica made no mention of her own plans. While Jackie dealt with her hair she talked only of Jackie's marriage, wanting every detail of the wedding.

'Can't say my first two marriages were a success!' she said above the noise of the hand hairdrier. 'Still, it makes a difference whether you marry for money or for love. Now, thank God, I have money of my own so I've decided to try my luck a third time.'

'You're going to be married again?'

The question came on an impulsive

note of surprise.

Veronica's brittle laugh rang out.

'Yes! That's why you're here, Jackie. I'm throwing an engagement party this evening — cocktails 6-9. I'd like you to stay, if you can.'

Jackie shook her head. She had never liked cocktails to drink and in any case, Chris would be arriving home from work.

'Ring him up and tell him to meet you here. I'll lend you something to wear. Now don't refuse me, Jackie. I've only met your husband once and I'd like to see him again. I'd also particularly like you to meet my fiancé.'

Jackie tried politely to refuse the invitation but Veronica swept aside her protests and reached for her telephone.

'I'll ring up your Chris and invite him myself, then he won't blame you for getting him involved. Besides, I hope it'll be a good party and there's masses of champagne and caviare. What's his number, Jackie? Now don't be stubborn! After all, you do owe me a favour in a way after the holiday I gave you.'

After that, Jackie felt she could no longer refuse.

True to her word, Veronica got on to the phone to Chris.

'Do say you'll come. Your bride is worried in case you might not want to, but if you'll come I know she'd be happy to join the fun.'

Chris had accepted. Put like that, he would not have refused if he thought it was something Jackie wanted.

'She's ruthless!' Jackie thought as she shut off the drier and began to unwind the rollers. 'She gets anything she wants just by ignoring other people's feelings — or using them.'

As she combed out Veronica's hair, the older woman said:

'You really do have a talent for hairdressing, Jackie. My hair never looks so nice as when you do it — even abroad. That's why I told Mr. Paul I'd pay him three times the usual. You're worth it, especially tonight. Don't laugh, Jackie, but I'm madly in love.

That sounds pretty flippant, but it happens to be true. This time my marriage is going to be really happy. There — that's the front door bell! Hurry up, I can't wait for you to meet the great man himself.'

Veronica dabbed some fresh powder over the careful layer of make-up Jackie had applied earlier and smoothed her hands over the skin-tight jersey material of her dress. Watching her, Jackie seemed to sense a new more exaggerated care for her appearance. Then Veronica turned suddenly and said:

'I'm crazy about him, Jackie. When you see him, you'll understand. Come on, I'm dying to introduce you.'

Jackie obediently followed Veronica down the thickly carpeted stairs. She had had no time to tidy her own hair or renew her make-up. She was still wearing the pale blue nylon overall she'd kept on beneath her coat when she'd left the shop. For the moment Veronica must have forgotten she'd promised to lend Jackie a dress to wear.

Jackie glanced at her wristwatch and saw that it was only half-past five. There would be time to change after she had said hullo to the fiancé. Suddenly, she came to a full stop on the bottom step of the stairs. Veronica had rushed ahead of her and had already reached the man standing in the doorway of the drawing room. All the colour drained from Jackie's face as she recognised him.

It was Antoine de Verre.

'*Darling!*' Veronica was drawling in her high-pitched slightly American voice. 'You know my little Jackie, don't you? Come over and congratulate us, Jackie. Why, you look as if you've seen a ghost!'

Veronica was staring at Jackie with an amused smile and did not see the angry flush of colour in Antoine's face, nor the sudden tightening of his mouth.

Jackie walked forward, her hand held out in a conventional greeting. She was still too shocked to find words. Veronica should have warned her . . . prepared her. Maybe she herself had been stupid not to guess.

'Mademoiselle Jacqueline!'

Antoine kissed her hand in Continental fashion. Veronica said quickly:

'Now then, Toni, no flirting. Jackie's a married woman these days and she's very *comme il faut.*'

'My felicitations,' Antoine said, looking deep into Jackie's eyes. 'I hope you are very happy with your Christopher.'

She raised her head quickly, defiantly and retorted:

'And I hope you'll be very happy, too, with Mrs. Cairgorn.'

Veronica was urging them both across the hall into the drawing room. At one end of the room was a miniature bar covered with bottles and glasses.

'What'll be, Toni? Jackie?' Her voice sounded gay and excited.

Jackie said breathlessly:

'I'll have mine later. I must go up and change my clothes. Will you both excuse me?'

She hurried from the room, Veronica's voice following her with instructions where she could find a cocktail dress and exhorting her to be as quick as she could.

Alone in Veronica's bedroom, Jackie sat down in the nearest chair and took a deep breath. Her heart was beating furiously, but not with any pleasure. She was strangely afraid. Not that Antoine could harm her in any way, but at the same time, she would have given her right arm not to have been forced to meet him again.

She shivered, and reaching in her handbag drew out a cigarette.

'How silly I'm being,' she told herself. 'He isn't interested in me now. He's going to marry Veronica!'

But that simply did not make sense. Veronica must be nearly twice Antoine's age — and besides she had already been married twice. Antoine was really still a boy . . .

No! That wasn't true. Antoine was very much a young man of the world — travelled, experienced, mature. Could he really be in love with Veronica? She was attractive in a hard, brittle way. When properly made-up she looked ten years younger than her age. Strange that Antoine had shown no interest in Veronica when they had first arrived at the hotel. Once or twice he had made some remarks about her to Jackie that were, if not exactly disparaging, at least faintly critical.

'Veronica should have warned me!' Jackie thought again, and then realized how silly she was being. Veronica had wanted to surprise them both, her and Antoine. It was not as if there had been anything between them — at least, nothing serious. She herself had repeatedly told Veronica that she was not interested in Antoine. Presumably it had not bothered Veronica that Antoine had once been keen on her, Jackie. Perhaps she had just written it off as of no account — as a bit of harmless flirtation on Antoine's part?

Slowly Jackie began to take off her overall. Some instinct forbade her borrowing a dress from Veronica. She didn't want to wear her clothes now. Instead, she would wear her own simple tweed dress which, if not exactly suitable for a cocktail party, was at least clean and smart. In any event, she would not stay for long. As soon as Chris came she would tell him she had a headache and ask him to take her straight home.

She took as long as she could over her hair and makeup, delaying the moment when she must return to the others. She was still lingering in the bedroom when the German maid came in with a message from Veronica telling her to hurry up and go down as the first guests would be arriving soon.

Jackie took a deep breath and followed the maid downstairs. She had nothing to be frightened of. She was behaving very childishly.

But Veronica was not in the drawing room when she went in. Antoine was there alone and rose at once to greet her.

'She has been called to the telephone,'

he explained. 'Now, *chérie*, let me get you a drink.'

Her woman's instinct warned Jackie that Antoine still found her attractive. His eyes followed her movements, and whenever she spoke to him she caught him looking deep into her eyes as he tried to hold her gaze.

She said coldly:

'I hope you and Veronica will be very happy.'

Antoine's eyebrows raised and he gave a shrug of the shoulders.

'That is without question. Veronique' — he gave the name its French pronunciation — 'is bringing me a dowry of half a million dollars. It would be difficult not to be happy with so much money.'

Jackie gasped. She was deeply shocked. At the same time she never doubted that he meant what he had inferred. He was marrying Veronica for her money. It explained everything.

Antoine was looking at her with an amused smile.

'There is nothing so awful in that, is there?'

'But she *loves* you!' The words came out involuntarily.

Antoine shrugged his shoulders again.

'That is her affair. She gets me — I get the money.'

'And she knows?' Jackie asked, astounded.

'Oh, *non!*' Antoine reverted to French. 'That would not be — how do you say? — *politique?*'

'I think it's horrible!' Jackie said, shivering despite the warmth of the room.

Antoine suddenly sat down beside her and imprisoned her hand against the brocade cushion.

'But then you think so many things are 'orrible. Now that you are a married woman perhaps you do not think sex is so 'orrible after all?'

He was teasing her, laughing at her, but she drew her hand away furiously.

'I prefer not to discuss such things with you.'

'But you were once a little in love with me.'

'No, no. I disliked you. Anyway, that is all past now.'

'But it is not past!' he said quickly, in a low, vibrant voice. 'I am still very much in love with you, my little Mees. Why do you not love me too? Veronique did not tell me you would be here tonight, but when I came to England last week I made up my mind I would find you somehow.'

'Please!' Jackie broke in desperately. 'This is ridiculous. I'm married now and I love my husband. Leave me alone. I don't want anything to do with you.'

'Still afraid of me? But you will not escape me, Jacqueline. We were meant for each other — I know it. One day we shared great joy and delight in each other. That day will come again. I know it. I can wait.'

Jackie jumped up and stood looking down into the sulky handsome face with loathing.

'I hate you!' she said childishly. 'I never want to see you again.'

Antoine did not seem upset. He looked quite pleased with the angry passion he had succeeded in arousing.

'And I love you. I dream of you every night. No other woman has behaved with me as you have done. No other woman has driven me to such determination. You will not be able to go on refusing me. I shall find a way — '

He broke off as Veronica suddenly came back into the room, her high stiletto heels tapping a warning on the polished parquet floor.

'Well, darlings!' she said, glancing from one to the other casually. 'Hope you've not been bored.'

'We were discussing the ski run from Cri d'Err to Crans,' Antoine lied with practised ease. 'I was telling Jacqueline that she must visit our hotel again next year.'

He stood up and walked over to Veronica, laying his arm across her shoulders in an intimate, possessive way she clearly appreciated. But her back was to him and she could not see Antoine's eyes staring past her into Jackie's flushed face.

'I must warn her somehow — warn her what he is really like,' Jackie thought, as she looked quickly away and down at her glass of sherry.

But she knew at the same moment that she could not do so. Veronica would not listen to advice from *her*. Besides, she wouldn't want to hear the truth. One had only to be in the room with her when Antoine was present to know that she adored him, and knowing Veronica's moral outlook as well as Antoine's, Jackie guessed that they were already lovers.

'Perhaps she'll get tired of him before they are married,' she thought. It could happen. But somehow she did not think so. No one knew better than she the strange attraction Antoine could arouse in women — an attraction of the senses that was sufficiently strong to overcome all scruples, decency and even love.

'Mr. Christopher Dershaw,' the German maid announced suddenly from the doorway.

Jackie jumped up and ran across the room into Chris's arms.

8

'Feeling better, darling?' Chris asked anxiously.

He was sitting on the edge of their bed, staring down at her white face with concern.

She tried to smile.

'I'm all right now. I think it's just tiredness and perhaps the drink I had on an empty stomach. Sorry to drag you all the way to Veronica's for nothing.'

Chris bent his head and gave her a quick kiss.

'I didn't mind, darling. By the way, who was the young man who came to the door with us? He sounded foreign.'

A faint colour stole back to Jackie's cheeks. She said quickly:

'That was Veronica's fiancé. He's Swiss.'

'He looked miles younger than she

does,' Chris remarked curiously. 'About half her age.'

'Yes, he is. She's forty-four and he's only twenty-two. She doesn't usually admit to more than thirty-five, but she told me once in Switzerland that she would be forty-five next birthday.'

Chris frowned.

'Doesn't sound quite right to me — not all that gap between them. Did you know him, Jackie? When he said goodbye I had the impression he called you by your Christian name.'

'Yes, I met him in Switzerland. I — I think I told you about him. His father owned the hotel.'

She wished Chris would not remain sitting on the bed. The directness of his stare made her nervous, and now — *now* was her chance to tell Chris about Antoine.

'You don't mean he was the one who took *you* out dancing?'

She nodded, the words sticking in her throat.

'But I don't understand. Why you? I

mean why not Mrs. Cairgorn?'

'I suppose because at that time she was busy with her own friends. And . . . and I was available. Chris he . . . he made a pass at me. I did try to tell you before, but . . . '

Chris, to her surprise, was smiling.

'Darling, you are a silly little goose — as if I expected anything else. Any man would find you attractive. Your lack of vanity is extraordinary. Don't you know how beautiful you are? He's probably marrying Veronica Cairgorn on the rebound.'

He was going to kiss her again, but she turned her face away and caught his hands, looking up at him with a kind of desperation.

'You don't understand,' she said. 'Antoine wasn't in love with me. I don't think he's the kind of man to fall in love. He's evil in some way — he's marrying Veronica for her money — he told me so. I don't think he has any morals at all. He wanted — '

She broke off, biting her lip. But

again Chris only smiled.

'So he wanted you. Darling, when will you understand that I don't mind how many men are attracted to you. In a way, it's a kind of compliment that I've got what so many other men want! I'm tremendously proud of you, darling. You musn't worry that I could be jealous. I'd only feel that way if I thought you were attracted to any other man. If that ever happened I don't know what I'd do. Thank God it hasn't ever happened yet. You've never given me a moment's unhappiness, Jackie, and my trust and faith in you are absolute.'

She was silenced as always by his implicit faith in her. She cried suddenly:

'But if I *had* been unfaithful? Supposing I had let a man like Antoine de Verre make love to me?'

Chris squeezed her hand.

'But you wouldn't. One of the reasons I love you so much is because you are different from most of the other girls. I've sometimes thought about the chaps who end up married to them. How must they have felt on their wedding night, knowing that some other man or men had come before them! I suppose I'm old-fashioned, but there's never been any other girl since I met you, Jackie, and I don't think I could bear it if there'd been anyone else for you other than me.'

For a moment she hated him. It was never easy living up to an ideal, and she longed to be able to cry out:

'But I'm only human. I wanted Antoine . . . I was horribly attracted to him . . . '

She would have given almost anything to hear Chris reply:

'But that's all right, darling. It happens to all of us!' That is what Rona would have said. *She* understood.

But Rona, who might have advised and protected her, was away from the shop with a heavy cold on the following day — the day Antoine decided to pay her a visit in the lunch hour.

It was young Sue who came running into the rest room, saying breathlessly:

'Oh, Jackie, there's ever such a handsome young man outside the shop. He asked me to come and tell you to hurry up — he said he'd been waiting half an hour already.'

If Rona had been there, Jackie would have asked her to go out and tell Antoine she most certainly did not wish to lunch with him. But Sue would never be able to handle Antoine.

She pulled on her coat and went through the now empty shop, Sue, following behind her, giggling excitedly.

Antoine opened the door for her, smiling.

'Ah, at last! I have been getting very hungry waiting here for you.'

He linked his arm through hers, ignoring Sue's stare, but Jackie drew her arm back sharply.

'I'm not lunching with you. I have an appointment . . . '

'Then you must break it. I have something very important to say to you.'

He looked so serious Jackie wondered if anything had happened between him and Veronica. For Veronica's sake she hoped Antoine had not broken their engagement — and yet it might be better for her in the long run . . .

Antoine took immediate advantage of her hesitation.

'I have booked a table at the Tudor Rooms. It is not very smart, but I could find nothing better. Come along, Jacqueline.'

She shrugged her shoulders and began to walk along the street beside him. The café where they were lunching was always very full . . . there could be no danger for her lunching with him. It might give her a chance to make him understand once and for all that she didn't want his friendship — or anything else from him. He must understand that whatever had been between them was over and finished and that she did not want to see him again.

Despite herself, Jackie was impressed

by the attention Antoine managed to receive. The head waitress hovered over them, taking great trouble with the order. Jackie and Rona had long since given up eating here, not only because it was expensive for their pockets, but because service was so poor and the waitresses overworked and bad-tempered. This one, however, seemed delighted to wait on Antoine. Jackie wondered if he could have given her a very generous tip in advance.

'Now!' said Antoine as they sat back to await the soup. 'Let us talk. Are you not a little curious *chérie*, as to how I found your salon?'

'I am more curious to know what is the important thing you have to tell me,' Jackie answered, ignoring the look in his eyes. She was not going to be drawn into a flirtation with him.

'Ah, yes! Well, I have to tell you that I am still desperately in love with you.' The smile left his face and he leant across the table, his eyes serious and narrowed. 'I have thought of nothing else but you since you left Switzerland.'

Jackie drew in her breath sharply. If she had been single and Antoine unattached, she might have been flattered. As it was, she felt only embarrassed and angry.

'You don't seem to understand the facts, Antoine. I told you from the first that I was in love with Chris. Now I am married to him and I love him even more. I would never, never be unfaithful to him. But even if he did not exist I would not want to go on seeing you. You seem to have forgotten you are engaged to Veronica.'

Antoine sat back in his chair and lit a cigarette. He blew the smoke into the air with a thoughtful expression.

'I was a fool!' he said, more to himself than to Jackie. 'I should have asked you to marry me there on the mountain when we were alone in the hut.'

'I would never have said yes!' Jackie said violently. 'I may have found you very attractive, Antoine, but I never *liked* you.'

He did not seem particularly hurt by her remark. He gave her a long searching look and then said quietly:

'All the same, I want you. I know, Jacqueline, why you ran away from the party last night. You are still afraid of me — afraid because I have a power over you.'

She flushed angrily.

'I'm not afraid of you. Why should I be?'

'Then it is your husband of whom you are afraid? Doesn't he know about me? Did you keep our secret from him, *chérie*? Perhaps he does not know you once gave yourself to me.'

'He loves me!' Jackie flashed back. 'There was no need to tell him anything.'

'So you would not mind if I wrote him a very nice letter, telling him how we spent the night alone on the mountain? Telling him how you lay in my arms, almost naked and oh, so beautiful, so desirable? I could tell him, too, of the hours we spent after the

200

dancing, alone in my car when you would kiss me and begin to tremble with the same longing as I had for you? I can tell him, too, of that evening when you at last became mine. Your wonderful Christopher who trusts you so much — he would believe that you didn't 'like me,' as you just said?'

Jackie's cheeks were scarlet. She was saved a reply by the arrival of the waitress, but she could barely eat the soup or the dishes that followed. Antoine ate in silence but his eyes seldom left her face. Jackie felt as if he were reading her thoughts, she didn't doubt that he knew he had succeeded in frightening her. Chris would never, never understand.

When the coffee came, Antoine said smoothly:

'I prefer not to force you, *chérie*. You know that. I want you to come to me of your own accord. But if you will not come, then I must make you.'

'You can't make me . . . ' Jackie began but broke off as she realized just what was happening. Antoine was blackmailing her. If she did not agree to see him again, he would get in touch with Chris and cause trouble.

'I could tell Veronica that you are marrying her for her money!' she said desperately. Antoine laughed.

'And so? I think Veronica knows this already. But she loves me too much to let this upset our engagement. No, you cannot harm me, Jackie, except by withholding yourself from me. I have arranged to take a little flat in London until Veronica and I are married. As soon as I have moved in, I will get in touch with you. You must come and visit me. It will be very private and we can be undisturbed.'

'I'll never, never do that!' Jackie said in a low fierce voice.

But back in the shop, alone with her thoughts, she realized just how difficult her position was. Either she must herself tell Chris about her affair with Antoine or she must comply with Antoine's wishes.

'I will tell Chris tonight!' she vowed. This time nothing would stop her confession. To do so might endanger Chris's love for her but not nearly so much as it would if he were to hear Antoine's version, or to find out that she had visited Antoine in his flat in London.

But that night Chris came home from work flushed with excitement at the news he had to tell her.

'Jackie, it's the most marvellous bit of luck. The manager called me in to his office today and was asking me about us. When I explained that we would have to go on saving another year at least before we could get our own home, he actually offered to lend us the difference.'

He swung Jackie round in his arms, laughing happily.

'Don't you see, darling, we can go out and buy our house now — tomorrow. And not only that, it shows what the manager thinks of me. It isn't to be a bank loan — but a private one between him and me. That means he trusts me. I'm on top of the world. This is one of the happiest days of my life!'

It was half an hour before he began to notice that Jackie was by no means as radiant as he was. He felt suddenly deflated and said:

'What's wrong, darling? You do want the house, don't you? You haven't changed your mind?'

'No, of course I want it!' Jackie said. Kind and tactful though her mother had been, she longed for her own home — somewhere where she and Chris would be shut off from the rest of the world; or entertain their friends. She tried to smile but her face felt stiff and she could think of nothing to say.

Alone in their bedroom several hours later, Chris was still making plans about the house. He seemed to have recovered his enthusiasm and to be utterly carefree. She couldn't bear to shatter his mood and yet she knew she *must*.

'Chris!' He broke off what he was saying to come across the room and sit down on the edge of the bed.

'Yes, darling?'

'I've got something to tell you — please let me say it and don't interrupt me. I've tried to tell you before, but . . . well, now I *have* to tell you. It's about that man you met yesterday — Veronica's fiancé.'

Chris looked down at her pale, averted face and the light went out of his own.

'Yes?' he prompted as she paused.

'When I was in Switzerland, I went out with him quite a lot. I — I wasn't in love with him but . . . but I found him very attractive.'

She tried not to notice the sudden withdrawal of Chris's hand or to hear the quick intake of breath that was almost a gasp.

'There was one night when we were halfway up a mountain — alone. I'd twisted my ankle. Remember I wrote and told you? It was terribly misty. We had to stay in a mountain hut for the night.'

Suddenly she raised her face and looked up at Chris in a desperate plea for understanding. But this time, it was he who looked away.

'Chris, nothing happened then — I give you my word . . . at least, nothing irrevocable. He . . . he did want to make love to me but . . . well, I didn't want to be unfaithful to you. I loved you, Chris . . . all the time I loved you. It was just that we were alone and . . . oh, I can't explain. There were other times, too, when I let him kiss me . . . touch me. I couldn't help it, Chris. I fought against it all the time but sometimes the feelings were stronger than my own will.'

She looked at Chris's white face in desperation. But his eyes were averted and he gave her no help.

'Chris! Please, please try to understand. I didn't love him — I didn't want to be unfaithful to you. But . . . one afternoon, I went again to the hut with him. When I agreed to go, I had no intention of letting him make love to me. It . . . it just happened. Chris, please, look at me . . . tell me you understand. It didn't really mean anything at all. It had nothing to do with my love for you.'

'Nothing to do with us?' Chris echoed. 'How can you say that?'

'Chris, it only happened once. Afterwards, I hated myself and him. I hoped I'd never see him again. Now — now he's here in England and he's trying to make me . . . oh, Chris, don't look like that . . . I don't like him, I don't want to see him again. I love you, I love *you*.'

The look on Chris's face frightened her. There was doubt there, and complete incomprehension.

'I don't think I quite understand,' he said slowly.

'I don't understand how it happened either!' Jackie cried, twisting her hands in her lap. 'I wanted to tell you when I first came back from Switzerland but you . . . you wouldn't let me.'

'Not *let* you?' Chris echoed, his voice

cold now and disbelieving.

'When I tried to talk about Antoine, you told me you trusted me absolutely and that made me feel so awful. I didn't want to hurt you, Chris . . . it seemed pointless to do so. It wasn't as if I had fallen in love with Antoine. I didn't even like him.'

Chris walked across to the dressing table and sat down. He picked up Jackie's hairbrush and ran his hands thoughtfully over the bristles. She wanted to run across the room to him, to hold him — make him understand somehow with the touch of her hands or her kisses. Even to her, her words sounded incredible.

'You said you didn't want to hurt me. Don't you see, Jackie — if you'd been honest with me about this — this affair, it would have been much easier to bear than the thought that you've concealed the truth all this time. Deceit is something I can't understand.'

'Oh, Chris!' She was almost in tears. 'I thought you might hate me . . . you *would* put me on a pedestal! You kept saying how perfect you thought me. I'm not perfect! I never was. I know it was wrong, but I just couldn't help the way I felt about Antoine.'

The words came out disjointed and high-pitched. She could feel Chris's lack of understanding but could see no way to bring him close to her again.

'There has to be more to it than you've admitted. One minute you tell me you don't like the man and the next you tell me you couldn't help the way you felt about him. What's it all about Jackie? I want to understand, but I'm afraid I can't.'

She drew in her breath. She said bleakly:

'I was attracted to him physically. I — I suppose I wanted to let him make love to me. But it was really you I wanted, Chris, only you weren't there and he was. Every time I went out with him, I swore I wouldn't go again and then the next night . . . I'm weak willed, I suppose.'

Chris's face was white as he swung round to stare at her across the bedroom.

'You told me you didn't love him — yet you wanted him to make love to you. You were too afraid to tell me about it when you came home. And yesterday — what about yesterday, Jackie? Was *he* the reason you ran out on that cocktail party? What kind of a hold has he got over you?'

'None, none at all!' Jackie said frantically. 'He threatened today to tell you about what happened between us if I didn't go to his flat — he was trying to blackmail me into going. That's why I had to tell you tonight. I — I hoped you'd understand and forgive me. Now you've heard the story from me, there is nothing more he can make me do. I need never see him again.'

'You saw him today?' Chris asked suddenly. 'When? What for?'

'He came to the shop and insisted I go out to lunch with him. I didn't want to but . . . '

'But he has such an attraction for you still that you had to go — just the way you kept going out with him in Crans?' Chris's voice was hard and accusing. Jackie cried:

'No, no, that's not true. I thought he wanted to talk about Veronica. I swear it, Chris. Since we've been married, I've never given him another thought.'

'And will you swear that, too?'

She was about to do so when suddenly she paused. It wasn't true . . . a strange fear of Antoine had gone on haunting her — had come between her and Chris. Now, if Chris would only understand, that would all be finished. She hated Antoine — hated him and everything he stood for.

'You don't answer. I suppose that is my answer. I am beginning to understand a few things now, Jackie. It's all beginning to make sense. There have been times when I've held you in my arms and felt that you were miles and miles away from me in your thoughts.

Now I see why. What I don't understand is why you married me. You didn't have to, you know, or am I wrong about that, too?'

'Chris!' She stared at him appalled. He *could* not believe she had married him because she feared the consequences of Antoine's love-making. He could not believe that.

As if aware of her thoughts, he said coldly:

'Well, is that so hard to believe? Or did you plan things so that there was no danger of a child?'

'Of course not! I told you it all happened on the spur of the moment. Chris, you can't think I would have cheated about a thing like that . . . '

'And why not.'

'Chris!' She was half crying with exasperation, and fear. They had never quarrelled like this — never been so completely apart in understanding. 'I married you because I loved you — you must know that's the truth. Why can't you believe me, Antoine had some kind

212

of fatal attraction for me — nothing more. My heart was never in danger.'

Chris gave her a long searching look.

'I'm sorry, Jackie, but it still doesn't make sense. I know you — you aren't the kind of girl who could muck around with men you didn't like. You may not like him now but at the time, you must have done so. Yet you never wrote a word about your feelings. If that doesn't indicate a guilty conscience, I don't know what does! And since then you've met him secretly for lunch. And what went on between you both before I arrived at Mrs. Cairgorn's house? Is that when you gave him your telephone number at the shop? 'Ring me there, Antoine, then my husband won't know anything about it'!'

Jackie gasped. This was a Chris she had never seen before. His face was flushed and his blue eyes hard and cold.

'He's jealous!' she thought, but the possibility gave her no satisfaction. She didn't want his jealousy — she wanted his understanding.

She was suddenly very angry with him. Until now she had been anxious to save him from disillusionment in her; to protect him. But now she felt that it was no longer only for Chris to forgive her; she, too, would find it hard to forgive him for believing the worst rather than the best in her. Because she had shattered his ideal, he was not prepared to let her remain partly on the pedestal. He wanted to debase her absolutely.

Silence hung heavy between them — a silence Chris, in his shocked state of mind, took to be Jackie's assent to her guilt. He didn't know what to do. Words no longer helped. He must have time to think.

'I'm going for a walk,' he said without looking at her. 'Don't wait up for me — I don't know when I'll be back!'

She half got to her feet, every impulse prompting her to stop him going. But suddenly pride forbade her to move. If Chris wanted to believe the worst of her, then he must do so. She had inadvertently hurt him but he was deliberately hurting her.

She sat perfectly still until the bedroom door closed behind him. Only then did she give way to tears.

9

'Two wrongs don't make a right, Jackie!' Rona said bluntly as they sat on their usual park bench eating a sandwich lunch.

Jackie's face was pale but determined.

'There's another proverb which fits the situation!' she said in a small, unhappy voice. 'It says one might as well be hung for a sheep as for a lamb.'

Rona frowned, lit a cigarette, and threw the packet to Jackie.

'But you don't *want* to go out with Antoine, do you? You told me you didn't like him!'

Jackie sighed.

'I don't much. But *he* loves me. Even you said you believed he was genuine enough about that.'

It was Rona who had had to turn Antoine away from the salon time and again these last two weeks, telling him at first Jackie was away ill and then she had decided to give up her job for good. Reporting to Jackie as she waited anxiously in the rest room, Rona had said:

'The poor man looked quite desperate. He kept saying, 'But I must see her somehow.' Of course, I could have told him to go round to your house, but obviously he daren't do that.'

There had been letters, too, arriving every morning at the salon and which Jackie, after reading the first, had put unopened in the waste paper basket.

The girls in the salon had been agog with curiosity and envy, too. Most of them had seen Antoine outside the salon and considered him exceptionally handsome. They questioned Jackie endlessly about him and refused to be put off by her non-committal replies. She had not dared to tell them that he was the rich Mrs. Cairgorn's fiancé since they would never have understood why he wasted so much time chasing Jackie.

Young Sue giggled and said to Jackie:
'What a pity you got married when you did — he's ever so handsome, real dreamy. I wish he'd go for me . . . '

Jackie could cheerfully have murdered him. She wanted only to be able to forget all about him, but he gave her no chance during the day, bothering Mr. Paul with phone calls and hanging round the door at closing time and in the lunch hour; and Chris gave her no chance to forget Antoine at home. Not that he ever spoke of Antoine — or spoke at all except for absolutely necessary conversation about a laundry bill or what time he would be back for supper.

The rift had gone on for two whole weeks. At first, Jackie had waited patiently for Chris to come round, at least to make the first move towards a reconciliation. But as the days and nights went by she began to give up hope. Clearly, she had just told Rona, Chris had fallen out of love with her. His ideal had gone.

'It was bound to happen sooner or later!' Jackie said bitterly. 'Perhaps it's for the best that it came now. Did I tell you Chris isn't buying the house after all. One of the few things he *has* said to me was to tell me he had reconsidered the loan his manager had offered us. I suppose it was his way of telling me our marriage is over.'

'It's all so silly,' Rona said in her placid sensible way. 'I can see how blindly in love Chris was — but he must know by now that you're flesh and blood the same as any other girl. Just because *he* wasn't tempted! And anyway, who knows he wasn't? He's never told you if he was so almighty faithful to you all those years you were engaged.'

'I suppose it's different for a man!' Jackie shrugged her shoulders.

'I don't see why!' Rona argued hotly. 'That's just it — your Chris doesn't seem to realize that times have changed and that kind of male privilege doesn't exist any more.'

The two girls smoked in silence for a minute or two. Then Jackie said:

'It was really all my fault. I knew how Chris felt about me . . . I ought to have told him about Antoine before I married him. Now it's all too late. He'll never forgive me. He thinks it was all far more important than it really was. Because I hid the truth from him, he assumes there *must* be more in it than I've told him.'

'He's behaving very childishly!' Rona said. And with a grin, she added: 'And so will you be if you persist with this idea of meeting Antoine again. All you are trying to do is to hurt Chris because you've been hurt.'

'Well, why not?' Jackie flared. 'In a way, he is as much to blame as I am when it comes to degrading our love. He's shown that his kind of love can't survive the first hurdle. Anyway, I don't intend to be unfaithful — only to lunch with Antoine — or perhaps to go out to dinner with him.'

'Will it stop there, Jackie?' Rona

asked astutely. 'You found him irresistible before, you know.'

Jackie pondered the question. With half her mind, she knew Rona was right — it could do no good seeing Antoine again. At the same time, she was not sure how much longer she could endure her present life with Chris. She still loved him. If he would make the smallest move towards ending the horrible rift in their marriage, she would rush to meet him. The silent evenings watching television were stretching her nerves to breaking point. Her mother, fantastic though it seemed, had not even noticed that anything was wrong. Since the wedding she had ceased to sit with them in the evening but always went to bed after supper. She had moved one of the big chintz covered armchairs into her room and neither Chris nor Jackie had been able to persuade her to join them.

'Young married people should have a chance to be alone together,' her mother had insisted. 'It won't last, you know. Soon there'll be a family growing up and you'll never have time to yourselves. Besides, I'm getting on — I like a bit of peace and quiet myself and I prefer the wireless to telly.'

So she wasn't present when they sat far apart in the brittle silence, never looking at each other but unable to ignore the other's presence.

It was the same in their bedroom. Jackie would go up first and Chris would linger over the boiler in the kitchen, or go out for a last walk down the street so that by the time he came up she was in bed reading a book or feigning sleep.

Jackie had begun to look pale and thin. Chris did not look well, either, but then unhappiness was never a promoter of good health.

'What does Chris mean to do?' Rona asked into the silence. 'Does he want a divorce, Jackie? And if so, on what grounds?'

Jackie's mouth twisted into a hurt grimace.

'I just don't know, Rona. Maybe

that's why I'm going to see Antoine again. Something has got to happen or I'll go out of my mind. Chris won't *say* anything and I can't ask him. If he wants me to go on living with him as his wife, then he'll have to tell me. This can't go on much longer. Don't you see, Rona, that my meeting Antoine again will bring things to a head. Chris will ask me if I mean to leave him, and I can tell him I don't want that but that I can't go on as we are.'

Rona nodded.

'I suppose it could work. But it does seem a long way round. Why not just ask him outright?'

'I did try — the day after the row!' Jackie said quietly. 'He wouldn't answer — he just looked at me and then turned and walked out of the room. I'm not going to throw myself at him, Rona. It's for *him* to tell me if he still loves me enough to want to stay married to me. I'm not going to beg Chris not to leave me. If he has stopped loving me I don't want him.'

Even as she spoke, she wondered if this was true. Deep down inside she did not believe that Chris would walk out on her. But if he did — then she knew she could never be truly happy again. But a fierce growing pride refused to allow her to think about the possibility for long, far less admit her fears to Rona.

It was pride, really, which finally induced her to meet Antoine. She did not altogether like the idea of going to his flat in the centre of London, but he told her on the telephone that he had an excellent housekeeper living in who would chaperone them.

'I give you my promise, *chérie*, that you need not be afraid. I want only to see you — talk to you.'

Jackie left a note, carefully drafted with much forethought, on the kitchen table where Chris would see it when he came in from work.

Chris,
I have gone to London to have dinner with Antoine. I really don't

particularly want to go, but it will be more amusing than sitting in silence with you. I shall be back by ten o'clock. Mother thinks I am visiting Rona and has promised to give you your supper. Jackie.

In the Underground her first misgivings began. Suppose when she got back Chris had packed his suitcase and gone? Suppose this act of defiance was all he had been waiting for to make up his mind finally to leave her? Suppose . . .

But it did not then occur to her to worry about the evening with Antoine. She thought she could manage him. It was not until she had been in his flat ten minutes that she realized the housekeeper he had mentioned was not there after all.

'I do hope you will not mind too much, *chérie*!' Antoine said, looking at her intently. 'You see, her sister is suddenly become ill and she asks me if I permit her to go on a visit. I cannot very well refuse, can I? Especially as she has left us the dinner all beautifully prepared.'

He saw the sudden colour in Jackie's face and the way she twisted her hands in her lap with that gesture now familiar to him which said she was unsure of herself. He turned away, a smile on his face he did not wish her to see.

'Now, let me get you another champagne cocktail. You look tired and a little unhappy. Nothing is wrong at home, I hope?'

Jackie looked round the luxurious apartment, only half-noticing the elaborate furnishings and beautiful furniture. To avoid answering his question she said quickly:

'This must be a very expensive place to rent, Antoine!'

He came across the room and sat down on a small footstool, his glass in his hand. He looked up at her with amused eyes.

'This is Veronique's engagement present to me. I have it for six months until we are married.'

Jackie gave a quick frown. She was shocked and yet not as much as she might have been hearing the same remark from anyone else. There was a disarming honesty about Antoine — a kind of boyishness in his expression which said, 'I know I am a naughty boy, but you will forgive me.'

'Poor Veronica!' she said aloud.

Antoine put down his glass, and taking away her own, took hold of both her hands.

'It is not for Veronique you should feel sorry, *ma petite*. It is for me. I am so very much in love with you and you are so cruel to me. For weeks I have been very patient and now at last you are here, alone with me. I am so full of happiness I cannot speak.'

The conversation was becoming too personal for Jackie's taste. She forced a laugh and said lightly:

'I don't imagine you are ever short of something to say, Antoine.'

'To you, no! I could speak for hours

on the mystery of your power. You are like no other woman I know — so calm and so — so unfeeling.'

'You know I'm not either of those things!' Jackie protested impulsively and then blushed again. She must not allow Antoine to make love to her verbally. Knowing him, it would not be long before he tried to kiss her.

'I'm hungry! Can't we eat now?'

Antoine, the true son of an *hotelier*, had ordered a banquet — oysters, smoked salmon, cold pheasant and marrons glacée as a sweet. With it he served several different wines which Jackie only sipped. Nevertheless, when at last he came in with coffee he had made himself, she felt her head whirling a little. She drank two cups of black coffee quickly but still did not feel clear-headed.

Antoine watched her covertly without seeming to do so. He had planned this little dinner party with the utmost care and attention. So far in his life no woman he had wanted had refused him so persistently. He had certainly never pursued any girl to her own country and then waited days, weeks, for one single chance to be alone with her.

Already he was bored with Veronica. She was typical of her kind and had nothing new to offer him once the novelty of a new conquest had worn off. But Jacqueline had a special fascination. Her very innocence was unusual in the crowd he usually mixed with, and she had not really lost that innocence with marriage. He knew that she could be passionate and that the cool poise was a very thin veneer covering a warm-blooded woman. He would not — could not — wait any longer. Tonight she would be his once more, and if he could but achieve this one night he was conceited enough to suppose that there would be others. He was, he considered coolly, an excellent lover. He sensed she had not yet forgotten the last time, despite her marriage.

If Jackie could have read his thoughts,

she would have gone home at once. But the effect of the different wines and the warm room and Antoine's apparent lighthearted manner had lulled her into a false sense of well-being. She was no longer afraid of him and felt she had convinced him over dinner that she would never be unfaithful to Chris, however badly he treated her. She had told him a little bit about their quarrel, and Antoine was all sympathy and understanding. It had soothed her bruised nerves and made her feel more than ever that any hurt Chris was now suffering he more than deserved.

Jackie began to enjoy her evening less when the phone suddenly rang. It crossed her mind that it might be Chris, but it was Veronica.

She could only hear Antoine's side of the conversation, but that was enough to disturb her as he lied easily and smoothly about his actions that evening.

' . . . but I have to go out at once, Veronique — I promised this man who wishes to do some business with my father. I am so sorry, darling . . . no, I have only just got in — I have been dining with some Swiss friends who are staying at the Savoy . . . '

When he rang off, Jackie stood up.

'I shouldn't be here,' she said flatly. 'It isn't fair to Veronica. She was always very kind to me and it really isn't fair.'

Antoine pushed her gently back on to the sofa.

'But no — I told you already I do not love her. She knows this and accepts this. She isn't interested in love — not love as you and I mean. She is only interested in bed.'

'Then why didn't you tell her you were here with me?' Jackie asked naively.

Antoine threw his hands up in the air with a Continental gesture.

'But she would not believe that we are sitting here talking like two good friends. She would imagine all kinds of things and be unhappy. It is best I tell a few fibs.'

Jackie relaxed. She could believe that

Veronica might be suspicious and jealous. All the same, she must go home soon. She had told Chris in her note she would be back by ten and it would take quite half an hour on the Underground.

It was half-past nine when she rose once more to go.

'This time I mean it, Antoine. I promised Chris.'

He stood up quickly, putting his arms round her and imprisoning her.

'Then break your promise. You cannot go yet, Jacqueline. First you must kiss me goodbye.'

She turned her face away, but he only held her more tightly. He was breathing quickly and she felt the first tinges of fear.

'One kiss! That is not so much. Once you liked to kiss me. Jacqueline — *je t'aime, je t'aime* . . . '

She began to struggle. Antoine only held her more tightly, trying to kiss her. She pushed with her hands against his chest, but knew at once that he was far,

far stronger and that she could not get free unless he released her.

'Let me go at once!' she cried. 'If you don't I'll scream!'

But Antoine's eyes only smiled, never losing their expression of determination.

'There's no one to hear you. Do not be silly, *chérie*. I will not hurt you.'

She fought him in earnest now, kicking and biting and sobbing, but she knew already that she was powerless to protect herself.

Antoine half-carried her, half-dragged her on to the sofa. There was a look of cruelty in his eyes which frightened her even more than the now unguarded look of desire. He was talking all the time in a mixture of French and English, but she was too distraught to listen. She thought:

'I was crazy to come . . . Rona warned me. Oh, Chris, Chris, help me . . . Why don't you come and help me.'

She bit hard on Antoine's hand as he began to tear the dress from her shoulders. He gave a little cry and then laughed.

'You are a woman of spirit — I like that. But this time . . . '

As if on cue the doorbell suddenly shrilled a warning.

'Chris!' Jackie gasped. Antoine's head was turned now to the door as he listened, an expression of angry frustration twisting his mouth as he swore volubly in French.

The bell rang again and as if released from a paralysis of fear, Jackie screamed.

Antoine stood up, straightening his clothing and said:

'Do not think you will escape me, Jackie. There will be another time . . . '

She ran past him and pulled open the door. But it was not Chris who stood there. It was Veronica.

Jackie burst into tears.

'I'm so glad you've come . . . oh, Veronica, he's horrible, horrible!'

She expected the older woman to put an arm round her comfortingly, but Veronica stood perfectly still, looking from Jackie's disarranged clothes across the room to where Antoine stood, sullen and narrow-eyed, staring back at her.

She walked past Jackie, ignoring her, and calmly poured herself a drink from the tray which stood on the coffee table. Then she said smoothly:

'Well, Antoine, perhaps you would like to explain?'

Jackie stared, unable to speak, as Antoine held out his hands to Veronica with a gesture of appeal.

'I am so glad that you are here, *chérie!*' he said evenly. 'I am afraid the situation is quite out of my control. I came back to my flat half an hour ago to find her' — he pointed to Jackie — 'waiting for me. I understand the hall porter let her in.'

Veronica sat down on the arm of the sofa, crossing her beautiful legs and staring down into her glass.

'And?' she prompted.

'And suddenly Jacqueline burst into tears and threw herself into my arms. I did not altogether understand what was happening, but it seems she quarrelled with her husband over me and when I tried to make her realize that you and I were soon to be married and that I had no interest in her, she became hysterical. I tried to make her leave the flat, but she only became more agitated and began to scream.'

Jackie's face was a furious red. She ran to Veronica and cried:

'But that's not true — none of it is true!' She began to explain what had really happened but Veronica cut her short.

'I am not interested in your lies!' she said coldly. 'I am well aware that girls of your sort are apt to throw themselves at Antoine — he's a very attractive man. Unfortunately, you had your chance and missed it. Now I suggest you go home and forget about this. After all, you are a married woman, Jackie. I'm sure your husband wouldn't like to know about this. If you bother Antoine again I shall feel it my duty to tell him.'

Jackie was too inexperienced and far too shocked to be able to think straight. She could not believe that Veronica doubted her — that she preferred to believe Antoine's version was the truth. But the look on Veronica's face was enough to tell her that more explanations were pointless.

She grabbed her coat and handbag and without a backward look at Antoine, hurried out of his flat.

As soon as the door had closed behind her, Antoine went forward to put his arms round Veronica, but the look in her eyes was cold and repelling. She said:

'I don't advise you to try that little game again, Antoine — not if you wish to marry me.'

He looked astounded and opened his mouth to argue.

'But you believed my explanation — ' he began when she interrupted him sharply:

'I let Jackie think I believed you. I am not quite such a fool as she is, Antoine, and the sooner you realize it the better. I'll put my cards on the table, shall I? I suspected you were up to something when you cut our date tonight. I thought it might be Jackie. I know you want her. But you aren't going to have her — *or any other woman*, Antoine. You will be utterly faithful to me and that is the price you will have to pay if you want to share my half-million dollars. So make up your mind. You can let me have your answer tomorrow.'

She stood up, and with a bitter little smile playing at the corners of her mouth she walked past him and out of the door.

Antoine stood looking after her, his mouth dropped open in an almost comical look of surprise and dismay.

10

Chris had been waiting on tenterhooks for Jackie to return. The clock's hands were dragging their way round to ten o'clock and he could not relax. Every few moments he got up and paced the room.

He knew that there must be a showdown. It was impossible for them to continue living as they had been these last few weeks. His health as well as his work was suffering, and Jackie, too, looked thin and desperately unhappy.

Her note had been a nasty shock. For the first time since their row, he had been made to realize that he might lose her. He kept wondering how they could have reached this state of affairs. What was it all about? Who had done wrong? Whose fault was it — his, or Jackie's? None of it made sense.

Until tonight a stubborn jealousy had

prevented him from seeing the facts clearly. Now, when it really looked as if Jackie had made up her mind to leave him, he saw that he might be the one to blame. It wasn't as if she had had a prolonged affair with that wretched Swiss fellow. He knew that. What he had been unable to stomach was the idea that she had been unfaithful to him. The idea had appalled him — his innocent, loving, perfect Jackie giving herself to another man.

He sat with his head in his hands, torn with conflicting emotions. He saw his pride in a new light. Deep in his heart he'd known that she'd never stopped loving him, that he ought not to mind about a purely physical weakness when all the time she had wanted him. He had been guilty of injured pride as well as jealousy, and had refused his wife the understanding he knew she would have afforded him in the same circumstances.

He had put her on a pinnacle and she had begged him time and time again to realize that she was only human. No wonder she had found it so difficult to tell him about the Swiss when she came home! He hadn't exactly made it easy for her, telling her all the time how much he trusted and admired her! He could see that now. When she came in he would apologize, tell her that they would forget the whole stupid thing and start again. Jackie was generous and forgiving. She would not want their marriage to break up . . . she loved him.

Or did she? He picked up the note and read it for the twentieth time.

I have gone to London to have dinner with Antoine . . .

Why? *Why* had she gone? Just to make him jealous? Or because she was still physically attracted to him?

She had also written:

I don't particularly want to go . . .

He clung to those words. She hadn't wanted to go. But suppose when she got there the fellow was amusing, charming, attentive — all the things Chris had failed to be these last few weeks. Maybe she could feel she had made a mistake — that she'd chosen the wrong man.

Now that it had come to this, he was at last able to sink his pride. When she came in he would fight with every word at his command to persuade her not to leave him. He would let her see how much he loved her . . . and how much he needed her.

He tried to envisage a life without her. Jackie had always been there — ever since his school days. In a way he'd always taken her love and her company for granted. Fool! Fool! he told himself. Pray God it was not too late.

But as the hands of the clock moved past ten he began really to be afraid. Maybe she wouldn't come back — maybe she had decided to burn her boats and stay the night.

Nervous anxiety had produced such an indescribable tension in him that when he heard Jackie's key in the front door he actually gasped. Relief was followed almost at once by anger. She had no right to torture him in this way.

She must have seen the light in the sitting room for she came in at once and stood blinking from a chalk-white face and huge shadowed eyes.

'Where have you been?' His voice was sharp with anxiety. She misunderstood his tone and took his words to be a reproof.

All the way home in the train she had felt numbed with shock and she had clung to the thought that Chris would be waiting for her at home. He would see how frightened she was, how upset. He would take her in his arms and everything would be all right again. But his pale, angry face seemed to her to be looking at her in an accusing way. He was probably only too anxious to believe the worst of her. Even Veronica had doubted her.

'With Antoine de Verre!' she replied with an effort, and gathering together her last remnants of pride, she swung round and left him alone again, staring after her.

His eyes had noted the untidiness of her hair and her clothes, and although he fought a swift inward battle to keep control of himself, jealousy swept through him once more like a white-hot flame. His distorted imagination saw only the worst. He felt sick. He could not be sure how far she had gone tonight alone with de Verre in his flat, but her face, her eyes, something about her struck him as weary and perhaps even a little guilty, as if she might be regretting what she had done.

Well, he told himself furiously, it was too late for regrets. This he would not tolerate. He had been a childish fool to suppose that Jackie had gone alone to a bachelor's flat merely for dinner! How she must be laughing at him, scornful because he was still in the house waiting for her when she chose to come home.

He hesitated for the fraction of a second, remembering the look on

Jackie's face. It was not exactly what could be called 'scornful.' It had been more distressed — almost shocked. Then his face hardened again. So she had got more than she had bargained for! Maybe that foreign boy friend of hers had lured her to his flat with promises of undying devotion and then showed her the door when she had finally given him what he really wanted.

He was too hurt and angry to feel any pity for Jackie. His imagination led him to picture quite clearly and certainly what had happened. He strode upstairs and flung open the bedroom door.

Jackie was lying on the bed fully clothed. Her face was turned into the pillow, but she was not, apparently, crying.

Chris paused, staring down at her angrily. She might at least look up and say something — that she was sorry . . . anything. But she never lifted her head.

'I'm packing!' he said with unconscious dramaticism.

Still she did not move, though he thought he saw a slight trembling of her shoulders.

'I'm leaving this house and you need not expect me to come back.'

He began to open drawers and cupboards and to throw his clothes into his suitcase with untidy abandon. All the time he half-hoped that Jackie would show some reaction — beg him to stay, give him a chance to reconsider the situation. If she were to cry — to show she was sorry, and above all, to show that she still loved him . . .

But Jackie was silent, her young figure lying rigid and unyielding on their bed.

When his packing was done, Chris paused once more in the doorway. He had no idea where he was going, or even if he could get a taxi at this time of the night. He knew he could not carry three heavy suitcases to the Underground and the buses would have stopped by now. He said:

'I'll send for my cases tomorrow.'

As Jackie did not lift her head or reply, he had no alternative but to walk out of the room with all the dignity he could muster.

As the front door banged behind him Jackie gave way to tears. She cried until her eyes were so swollen she could not see.

Her mother knocked on the door and came in.

'I thought I heard the front door . . .' she began and then noticing that Chris was not there and that Jackie was still lying fully clothed on the bed, she hurried to her daughter, saying:

'Oh, darling! Have you and Chris had a row?'

It was some moments before Jackie could speak. Her mother sat on the bed, stroking her head until she was calm enough to say in a hoarse little voice:

'Chris has gone. He's never coming back. Oh, Mother . . .'

'Now, now, dear! All young couples have rows. You musn't upset yourself so.

Chris loves you. He'll be back. You'll see, Jackie, in the morning he'll be round full of apologies. No doubt he's already regretting whatever he's said to make you so unhappy.'

'But it wasn't Chris's fault . . . it was mine!' Jackie wept.

'Do you want to tell me about it?' Mrs. Kemster asked gently. But Jackie shook her head. Her mother couldn't possibly understand. She would be as shocked and disillusioned as Chris had been, and Jackie couldn't bear to lose her mother's good opinion and love now when she was so alone.

While her mother went down to the kitchen to get a hot-water bottle and brew a cup of tea, Jackie lay thinking about Antoine and Veronica. Only now did she wonder what had brought Veronica to her fiancé's flat when he had expressly told her he'd be out. Had she suspected something? Yet, if she had suspected Antoine why did she blame her, Jackie, for what had happened, apparently only too eager to accept

Antoine's version. It didn't make sense. Nothing made sense any more.

Jackie tried to feel comforted by her mother's certainty that Chris would telephone or turn up next morning. But deep down she did not expect him to do so. She had seen the look on his face and she knew him well enough to realize that he would never have left the house unless he meant it to be a permanent break.

She was not well enough to go to work in the morning. Her mother telephoned Rona and asked her to tell Mr. Paul she would not be in. Mr. Paul would not be pleased, since she was fully booked with clients for the day, but Jackie's face was still swollen from crying and she was utterly exhausted.

Mrs. Kemster wanted to get the doctor, but Jackie was adamant. She knew no doctor could cure unhappiness.

She slept on and off during the day and was woken by Rona with a cup of tea at six o'clock.

Rona smiled cheerfully at her friend as she sat on the edge of the bed, hiding the shock she felt at the sight of Jackie's face.

'Your Mum said I could come up. You don't mind?'

Jackie shook her head. Any company was better than lying alone with one's thoughts and to Rona she could explain.

Rona listened carefully, smoking and drinking tea. The room was warm, and for the first time since Chris had left, filled with a feeling of companionship.

When Jackie ended her story, Rona said:

'I had a feeling you were on the wrong track!' She gave Jackie a smile and added — 'The trouble with you, Jackie, is that you are far too soft. You should toughen up a bit — get wise!'

'Well, what would you have done in my place?' Jackie asked curiously. 'I agree I've made a ghastly mess of everything, but I can't see how it could have been any different.'

Rona sighed.

'Probably not, since you are very much you. If I'd been in your shoes and supposing I'd met Antoine in Switzerland, I'd probably have given way to the basic urge, too. But it was all wrong for *you*. Frankly, I think it's a pity you ever met the man. You aren't the type who can have your cake and eat it. Some girls, like me, can flit through life just taking the good things as they come along and not really *caring* very deeply. It's different for the intense ones like you.'

'You think I take life too seriously?'

'Not necessarily. But Chris is making far too much of your one and only misdeed. I'll bet my bottom dollar you aren't the only woman your Chris has held in *his* arms. When it came to a showdown about Antoine, did you ask Chris if he'd been such a model of good behaviour? I'll bet you didn't!'

Jackie shook her head.

'There you are then! *I* wouldn't have told Chris anything — I'd just have forgotten the whole affair.'

'I couldn't!' Jackie said desperately. 'It — it preyed on my conscience so that even when Chris made love to me I'd be thinking about Antoine. I had to tell him.'

'And shove your feelings of guilt on to poor old Chris! Mind you, I blame him, too. It's not fair for any man to idolise his woman. We are all human, whatever he may want to think. Perhaps if you'd been a little less perfect to begin with he wouldn't have expected such perfection at the end,' Rona said. 'Personally, I don't believe in long engagements. The tension was bound to get too much for you. Chris should have recognized the fact.'

'And now it doesn't any of it matter. I don't suppose I'll see Chris again.'

Rona looked at her friend intently.

'Why not? Don't you want to see him? You're not, I hope, feeling guilty about last night?'

'No! But Chris won't come back. I know him.'

'Then *you'd* better go and find *him*.'

'But I can't!' Jackie cried. 'If he doesn't want me, I — '

'Who said he didn't want you? Did he? This is no time to stand on your pride, Jackie. If you want him, *go and get him*. And don't go telling him how sorry you are and start begging him to forgive you.'

Seeing Jackie's puzzled expression, she laughed.

'Get angry with him — if you can! Tell him just exactly what happened last night and then say he can like it or lump it but that's the truth. He'll believe you. You've such a revealing face, Jackie, no one could possibly doubt you.'

'And if he doesn't care any more?'

'Then he is not worth your love or your heartbreak!' Rona said flatly. 'Damn it all, Jackie, he married you and he promised to love and cherish you in bad times as well as good. Look what's happened at the first hurdle! Chris walks out. He's the one who has failed since your marriage — *not you*. Make him see that. Make *him* ask *you* for forgiveness.'

For a moment Jackie looked more cheerful, but then she said:

'Chris will never understand why I went to Antoine's flat last night. It even seems crazy to me now. I suppose I wanted to make Chris jealous.'

'Then tell him. He'd have seen that for himself if he'd not been so blinded by jealousy.'

They were still talking about Chris when the phone rang. A few minutes later Jackie's mother appeared in the door. She looked at Jackie anxiously and said:

'That was Chris, darling. He . . . he wouldn't let me get you to the phone to talk to him. He asked me not to tell you he telephoned.'

Jackie looked at her mother, bright-eyed with hope.

'He's coming back?'

'I'm afraid not, darling. He said he was coming round in twenty minutes for his suitcases and would I have them ready by the front door as he didn't want to come in. He made me promise not to tell you, but — '

'You were quite right — and a good sport!' Rona said warmly. 'Sounds to me as if Chris is scared to face you, Jackie. Thinks he'll lose what little determination he has to go through with this if he catches sight of your dear little face!'

Jackie looked from Rona to her mother helplessly. She no longer knew what was best. Rona was the only one who seemed capable of handling the situation.

'It's far too good an opportunity to miss!' Rona was saying enthusiastically. 'You must contrive to be downstairs when he calls, Jackie. You've just *got* to.'

'But I can't!' Jackie said. 'I'm not like you, Rona. I wouldn't know what to say. He'd only start arguing again and . . . oh, Rona, I couldn't stand it. You don't seem to realize that I love him.'

'I realize it!' Rona said grimly. 'The

one who has to be made to is Chris.'

'Shall I talk to him, dear?' her mother asked. She was not quite sure what had happened between Jackie and her son-in-law, of whom she was very fond, but she was willing to do anything to put things right.

'No, I will!' Rona said, ignoring Jackie's protests. 'This time leave things to me, Jackie. Will you?'

Jackie had suddenly turned very white. She said:

'I think I may have to, Rona. It's probably nerves, but I think I'm going to be sick.'

Jackie was still in the bathroom, her mother holding her head, when Rona heard the taxi stop outside the front door. She ran downstairs and flung open the door, pulling a surprised Chris into the hall.

'I want to talk to you,' she said firmly. 'Come into the sitting room.'

Chris drew his arm away.

'I can't stay, Rona,' he said, glancing up the stairs. 'I've asked the taxi to wait.'

'Then tell him to go,' Rona said. 'We can ring for another if you still want one when I've finished talking. Please, Chris — it's important. Jackie's upstairs and refuses to come down, so you needn't be afraid you're going to see her.'

He hesitated for a moment longer, then shrugged his shoulders.

'All right!'

He went outside and paid off the taxi. When he went into the sitting room, Rona was already sitting by the fire. Chris sat down opposite her and said wretchedly:

'It's a hell of a mess, isn't it?'

'There's nothing gone wrong that can't be put right,' Rona said. 'At least, not if you are willing to listen to reason.'

Chris stared down into the fire, his eyes clearly showing the depth of his unhappiness.

'It can't be put right this time, Rona. This time it has gone too far.'

11

Rona lit a cigarette and tossed the packet over to Chris.

'I wouldn't have suspected a bank clerk had such an imagination!' she said with a half smile. 'The trouble is, Chris, you don't *know* how far things have gone. *But I do.*'

Chris looked uncomfortable.

'I know you mean well, Rona, but really, I'd rather not hear any of Jackie's confidences!'

'Don't be such a prig!' Rona replied unconcernedly. 'You said you'd listen to what I have to tell you and you shall. You're all wrong about Jackie. I'm not sure that she isn't far, far too good for you. In any case, I don't see what right you've got to demand perfection. Has your life been blameless? And don't look like that. I know it isn't my place to be saying this, but Jackie never will.

She's the one who should be here telling you a few home truths.'

She paused and then drew in her breath.

'So far, Jackie has been completely faithful to you. Moreover, she had to endure a very nasty experience last night purely because you were behaving so childishly that you forced her into an equally childish form of retribution. She didn't want to go to that man's flat in the first place, Chris. She told me beforehand. The object of the exercise was to make you jealous — force you into talking to her.'

'She didn't have to go to those lengths to — to talk to me,' Chris argued. 'Why didn't she just say she wanted to have it out?'

'Because she was quite convinced you had stopped loving her. The rift was of your making, Chris, not hers.'

Chris's face looked flushed in the firelight.

'Last night I was going to make it up . . . tell her we'd forget everything and make a fresh start.'

'So her plan would have worked!' Rona remarked pointedly. 'She made you sufficiently jealous to come off your high horse.'

'I wasn't jealous — ' Chris began but broke off. It was true after all. He'd been eaten up with jealousy and when Jackie had come home so late, looking as she had done, he'd been convinced of her guilt.

'It's all too late for explanations,' he ended coldly. 'She can't love me if she can go and behave like that with a man who . . . *it's too late*, Rona.'

Rona sighed.

'So you still want to believe the worst of her. Don't you know your own wife, Chris? Jackie's so pure in heart, as the saying goes, that she felt she'd committed a dreadful crime because she let another man make love to her *before you were married, too*. Can't you see that it was partly your fault she did so? Long before she went to Switzerland she was finding things tough. She wanted to get married, but *you* didn't. You wanted to wait till you had enough money to set up house the way *you* wanted. Jackie didn't care . . . she told me so. She had had three years of loving you, Chris — a love which was never satisfied. I don't know how you coped with your emotions, but Jackie wasn't finding it easy to cope with hers. You should have married her, Chris. At least you should not have urged her to go off on a holiday with a woman like Veronica Cairgorn without you. She didn't even want to go. She was hurt and resentful because you kept telling her to go off and leave you and enjoy herself. Have you the right to blame her when she did?'

Chris swallowed.

'I suppose it seems silly to say I trusted her.'

'What right had you to shackle her? You put your feelings before hers. You wanted money — not just enough to keep her as your wife but to have a home all furnished down to the last curtain and carpet. Until you had what *you* wanted she could sit and curb her natural desires. If anyone has been selfish — if anyone has been to blame — it was you, Chris.'

Chris felt slightly sick. He was no longer sure who was right — who wrong. All he knew was that he couldn't go on living the life he had shared with Jackie these last weeks. Night after night he had lain awake, tormented with thoughts of her lying in another man's arms, thoughts of another man taking what was rightfully his.

'Think it over, Chris! It's probably the last chance you will have to make a go of your marriage. I'm going to put the kettle on.'

Left alone, Chris sank down in the chair by the fire and lit a cigarette. He was ashamed to see that his hands were trembling. In a way, Rona's words had brought home the truth. This wasn't a game of wits between him and Jackie; this wasn't just a quarrel any more. He had to decide whether he wished his marriage to go on.

He was adult enough to know that the decision was his; mature enough to realize that it wasn't just a question of what he *wanted*. He wanted Jackie; wanted to stay married to her. But what kind of marriage would it be when every time he took her in his arms he felt a searing flame of jealousy for Antoine de Verre, for stealing his wife's innocence. What hope had they of happiness if he couldn't forget the past.

Rona had said, 'Until you had what *you* wanted Jackie could sit and curb her natural desires.' Deep down inside he knew that was fair criticism. He remembered how often in those days before Jackie went to Switzerland she had begged him to forget about 'his little black accounts book' and get married. He remembered, too, with a strong feeling of unease, how he had had to call a restraint on their love-making for fear that they would lose control. He ought to have realized that a warm-hearted, passionate, loving girl like his Jackie could not put a permanent curb on her emotions. It wasn't even as if they had set an actual date for their wedding so that they could say to each other: 'We must only wait for a few weeks, months longer.'

When Rona came back, Chris said quietly:

'Are you sure she isn't in love with de Verre?'

'She hates his guts!' Rona said crudely. 'He's the one who has made all the running — Jackie has only run away. He wanted her all right — so much so that he tried to force her against her will last night in his flat. Fortunately for Jackie, Veronica Cairgorn had some sixth sense warning and turned up at the flat just as Antoine had Jackie pinned down on the sofa. Jackie ran home then — and to what? For you to take one look at her and then pack your bags and walk out. Poor little devil was nearly scared out of her wits.'

Chris was staring at Rona with horrified eyes.

'And is this true?'

'Absolutely! Jackie was actually forced to fight him. Somewhat surprisingly, Mrs. Cairgorn chose to believe Antoine's story, which was that Jackie had thrown herself at his head and become hysterical when he had refused her. Even with your imagination, I can't see *you* believing that of Jackie. It's my bet Veronica didn't believe it either. But she wants the young man and she couldn't very well keep him and believe Jackie's version, could she? Can't say I envy her — she's going to have a rotten life with him.'

Chris's hands were over his face.

'Poor Jackie!' he was saying. 'My God, poor Jackie!'

Rona looked at him without pity but with plenty of satisfaction.

'I'm glad you're coming to your senses at last. 'Poor Jackie' spent all last night in tears — two shocks in a few hours were a bit too much for her. Now she's ill and I don't wonder. What are you going to do about it?'

He was on his feet ready to rush upstairs, but Rona stood up and put a hand on his arm.

'I don't know if she will see you!' she said, deviating for the first time from the truth. She calmed her conscience with the thought that Jackie would never be able to make Chris eat humble pie. She might as well do the job properly.

'After all, you treated her pretty rottenly from the start. First you made an almighty scene about the silly goings-on in Switzerland. Perhaps that was excusable. But then you made another jealous scene about her lunching with him, and lastly you walk out on her at the moment when she needs you most. You can hardly wonder if she doesn't feel like falling into your arms at this moment.'

Chris looked at Rona desperately.

'But she must see me! I've got to tell her how sorry I am. Even if she doesn't want to go on living with me, I must at least have a chance to say I'm sorry — to beg her to forgive me.'

Rona appeared to hesitate. Then she said:

'Well, wait down here. I'll go up and see if I can persuade her.'

Chris was appalled. He never doubted Rona's story. Now it all made sense and his own behaviour seemed incomprehensible. He had spent a miserable night in the station hotel where it was dirty and uncomfortable, longing to come home and yet allowing his stupid pride to restrain him. He'd hardly done a stroke of work at the bank and had even reached the point of deciding to go out and get drunk rather than face an evening alone in that horrible hotel. Finally he had decided to go round to the house for his suitcases, not realizing that deep down he was half hoping to catch a glimpse of Jackie and somehow, even at the last minute, patch things up with her.

Rona sat on Jackie's bed fighting a losing battle.

'Don't you see, you silly goof, that it will do him all the good in the world to leave him stewing till morning? I don't care if he is unhappy — he deserves to be. You can weaken in the morning, if you must, and ring him up.'

'But, Rona, I can't do that. I want to see him now. It was my fault, too . . . I was stupid and . . .'

Rona flung her arms in the air.

'I give up — you're impossible, Jackie. Now I've got him eating humble pie and you want to fall into his arms saying it was all your fault.'

Jackie smiled tremulously.

'Well, it was! Oh, Rona, please — send him up. If you don't, I'll get up and go down to him.'

'I think you'd better stay to supper, Rona, dear,' Mrs. Kemster put in quietly. 'Perhaps you'd like to come and help me get it ready. I'm sure Chris must be hungry and Jackie must be quite empty. Do you think you could eat something, dear?'

Suddenly she was hungry — hungry and happy. Chris loved her — he still loved her, and that was the only thing in the world that mattered. *Their marriage wasn't breaking up after all*. It was really just beginning. She felt so full of happiness and excitement that her heart was thundering inside her. It was as if this — and not that other day — was the start of their honeymoon.

Hurriedly, she jumped out of bed and ran across to the dressing table to powder her face and put on lipstick. Then she heard Chris's footsteps on the landing and his voice outside the door saying softly:

'It's Chris, Jackie. May I come in?'

Despite the make-up she looked pale and tired as Chris slowly approached the bed. She looked at him nervously and then her gaze swung away and down to her hands.

'Jackie?'

He sat down on the edge of the bed and took one of her hands in his, holding it tightly.

'Darling, I'm so very sorry. I've behaved very badly. Can you forgive me? Can we make a fresh start?'

She was crying silently, hopelessly. Chris could not bear the sight of her tears.

'Darling, don't. Please don't. I've been a brute, I know, but I swear it'll be all right if you'll give me another chance. Jackie, look at me. Please!'

She cleared her throat and tried to speak. At first the words were choked, but presently she said clearly:

'A little while ago I felt if only you would come back everything would be all right. Now I know it won't — *not ever.*'

'Jackie, you can't say that — you mustn't. Surely you can forgive me. You haven't stopped loving me altogether.'

Jackie covered her face with her hands.

'Don't you see, Chris, it has nothing to do with my loving you. Of course I love you. I've never loved anyone else and I never will, but our marriage is finished. It ought never to have been at all. I had no right to marry you in the first place.'

Chris's face began to take on more colour. He took Jackie firmly by the shoulders, forcing her to look at him.

'Best say now exactly what you mean, darling. Let's have it all out in the open once and for all. Then we can forget it and start again.'

'That's just it!' Jackie said desperately. 'We won't be able to forget. You won't and I won't. It'll always be there between us, spoiling everything. Oh, Chris . . . ' her voice broke on a fresh flood of tears.

'Jackie, this is all nonsense. I worked it out just now when I was alone downstairs. Whatever happened *before* we were married was as much my fault as yours. I know that now. I'm not going to try and pretend I wasn't terribly shaken when you told me what had happened in Switzerland. I had put you on a pedestal, and I suppose, since we are being absolutely honest with each other, that I was forced to realize you did not belong there. But you were not my wife at the time and you committed no crime. I had no right to complain at anything you did.'

'That's not true!' Jackie cried. 'We were engaged, Chris, and more than anything in the world I wanted to be married to you. What I did was wrong on two counts — because of our engagement and because I didn't love him — I didn't even like him very much. I gave way to a purely physical appetite and I'm so ashamed. I knew I would hate myself for it and I have . . . ever since. *You* weren't weak, Chris . . . and I was.'

Chris stood up and walked to the window. Jackie could not see his face as he said quietly:

'No, darling, I was weak, too. I nearly told you once — there was a typist who . . . '

'Oh, Chris! Don't tell me. I don't want to know.'

He stood shamed and yet glad that he had had the courage to speak. Now that the whole truth was out he could see even more clearly that he, least of all, had had the right to judge Jackie. It was curious how at the time he hadn't thought a great deal about his own act of unfaithfulness while Jackie was away. It had meant nothing at all — to him or to the girl who had a reputation known to all his colleagues. It had been a cheap, meaningless episode — one he had preferred to forget. But it had happened, and was there really so much difference between his behaviour and Jackie's? Because she was a woman and, until Switzerland, had been inno- cent, it had seemed to him that she had done something terrible. Yet his own actions had caused him no more than a passing memory of distaste.

'You say you can forgive me!' Jackie was saying quietly. 'But I'll never forgive myself.'

'You will!' Chris said, suddenly sure of himself and the future. 'It is because of the way I've behaved that the whole thing has assumed such importance. We're going to forget it, Jackie — forget it ever happened, forget that man ever existed. We've neither of us ever loved anyone else and *that* is what matters. The past is buried — we'll bury it now together. It is the future that matters now.'

He sat down once more beside her and took her gently in his arms. At first her body was stiff and unresponsive and then she clung to him with a fierce desperation.

'Make me believe it! More than anything in the world I need to believe it!' she cried.

'It's forgotten already!' Chris whispered against her lips.

But Jackie knew that life was never quite so simple. There would be times when she remembered, even if Chris forgot; times when in the darkness she knew she would remember and regret that Chris had not been the first and only lover in her life.

Perhaps, she thought, as Chris's warm, loving hands caressed her, there were girls to whom her own experience would have meant nothing at all. She knew that Rona and many of the girls at the salon thought nothing of sleeping with their boyfriends when they wanted to. She knew, too, that it wasn't just a question of the right standard of behaviour, or morals; those standards had been created by older, wiser people to protect girls like herself from the unhappiness they could create for themselves if they ignored them. It wasn't 'wrong' just because convention said so. It was wrong because the fullest expression of love could be beautiful only between a man and woman who truly loved one another. And for her, Jackie, there was only ever one man — Chris.

Downstairs in the kitchen, Rona stirred the sauce she was making and said thoughtfully:

'What an emotional girl Jackie is. It's a pity she isn't a bit more placid — like me. I don't think I've ever been sick from nerves in my life.'

Mrs. Kemster lit the gas beneath the potatoes and looked at Rona with a mysterious little smile.

'Nor has Jackie!' she said. 'Not even when she was a very little girl.'

'Then why — ' Rona began, and stopped, her feminine intuition helping her to divine Mrs. Kemster's thoughts. 'Oh, no!' she said. 'Not a baby! Does Jackie know? Will she be pleased? Will Chris want one?'

Mrs. Kemster folded her arms in a satisfied way and replied:

'I don't think Jackie knows yet. Of course, I could be wrong — but I don't think so. I didn't say anything just now when the thought crossed my mind. I thought it might be better to let the two of them sort themselves out first. After all, it may be the last chance they have to be . . . well, just the two of them alone.'

'And you think they'll be pleased?'

'I'm sure they will!' said Mrs.

Kemster confidently. 'After all, a baby will give them every excuse to move into that home Chris has always wanted. And besides, it's natural for a woman to want a child by the man she loves.'

Rona nodded.

'That's true!' she said. 'I think I'll start Pete thinking about marriage. We could afford it now.'

Jackie lay in Chris's arms. She felt a new quiet happiness and Chris touched her hair lightly with his lips.

'We'll move into the new house next month — I'm sure the manager will still give me that loan. Oh, darling, just think — we'll be quite alone together at last. When we shut the door it'll be on our own little world — nobody in it but you and me.'

A tender little smile played round Jackie's mouth. Silently she raised her face and returned his kiss.

We do hope that you have enjoyed reading this large print book.

Did you know that all of our titles are available for purchase?

We publish a wide range of high quality large print books including:
Romances, Mysteries, Classics
General Fiction
Non Fiction and Westerns

Special interest titles available in large print are:
The Little Oxford Dictionary
Music Book, Song Book
Hymn Book, Service Book

Also available from us courtesy of Oxford University Press:
Young Readers' Dictionary
(large print edition)
Young Readers' Thesaurus
(large print edition)

For further information or a free brochure, please contact us at:
Ulverscroft Large Print Books Ltd.,
The Green, Bradgate Road, Anstey,
Leicester, LE7 7FU, England.
Tel: (00 44) 0116 236 4325
Fax: (00 44) 0116 234 0205

Other titles in the
Linford Romance Library:

THE ECHOING BELLS

Lillie Holland

In Germany Marnie Burness accepts the post of governess at Schloss Beissel. Her charge is Count von Oldenburg's daughter, Charlotte. Despite finding much to disapprove of at the Schloss, against her own principles she falls in love with the Count. Then, when Maria, the Count's wife, is murdered Marnie suspects his involvement. She leaves the Schloss, but will she ever learn the truth about the death of the countess — and will her suspicions of the Count be proved right?

THE ORANGE MISTRESS

Sara Judge

Alice Wingard tells the story of how Nell Gwyn saves her from destitution when she is orphaned. Nell takes her to live in a bawdy house in Coal Yard Alley. The well-educated Alice finds her new surroundings shocking. Yet the girls' friendship deepens as, together, they move on from the theatre in Drury Lane, to Pall Mall and then to the court of the lascivious Charles II. Sharing happiness and sorrow, they encounter bloodshed, passion and political intrigue . . .

ELOPING WITH EMMY

Liz Fielding

Emerald Carlisle's father will do anything to stop a wedding between her and her penniless friend Kit Fairfax. Announcing their engagement seems a sure-fire way of helping Kit raise some cash! Tom Brodie is her father's lawyer. His duty, to buy off the groom and to bring Emerald to heel, is thwarted by Emerald's beauty and charm. When she persuades him to help her 'elope', Tom soon realises she could persuade him to take her anywhere . . . even up the aisle!

KISS OF YOUTH

Denise Robins

When Judy Grant's car broke down in the country, miles from anywhere, she little imagined that the handsome man who came to her aid was her future employer's husband. Nor, indeed, did Richard Portal realise that the girl he had rescued — and fallen helplessly in love with — was his own wife's cousin. It seems that their love is doomed — until the unexpected happens, offering them a chance for happiness greater than they have ever known . . .